GHOSTS OF ORDINARY OBJECTS

The Truce

ANGIE SMIBERT

BOYDS MILLS PRESS
AN IMPRINT OF BOYDS MILLS & KANE
New York

Boyds Mills Press
An imprint of Boyds Mills & Kane, a division of Astra Publishing House
boydsmillspress.com

Printed in the United States of America
ISBN: 978-1-62979-852-3

Library of Congress Control Number: 2019950728

First edition

10 9 8 7 6 5 4 3 2 1

Design by T. L. Bonaddio
The text is set in Adobe Garamond Pro.
The titles are set in Aviano Sans.

To all the Forever Girls—and Forever Boys—out there

December 1942

BIG VEIN, VIRGINIA

THE FADED YELLOW PICKUP, its paint now almost white as sand, puttered up the mine road to the boardinghouse. Small wet flakes of snow melted on Bone's tongue as she sat on the front steps, watching the truck's progress. The snow barely left a skift of cover before it melted into the brown grass. Up the road at the church, the choir practiced "O Holy Night."

Bone Phillips pulled her mama's butter-yellow sweater tight around her. As her fingers dug into the yarn, it showed her mother unwrapping a sparkly pink ornament. She handed it to her sister while a very young Bone and her cousin played nearby. Daddy and Uncle Ash dragged an enormous Virginia pine into the parlor of their old house. Mama inhaled the scent. Pine tar and damp earth mingled with fresh-baked sugar cookies, filling the tiny room. The men raised the tree up in the corner, only to find the poor thing a foot too tall. Mama laughed, and Bone felt her pure joy in the moment.

"Stop it, Mama," Bone whispered as she pushed the vision away. Mama might have been dead for six years, but she wasn't above nudging Bone out of a mood.

This Christmas wasn't going to be joyous—or peaceful. How could it be? Daddy was off to war, fighting Nazis somewhere in North Africa. Uncle Henry's ship went down not two months ago in the Atlantic. Ruby was moving to Radford. And it was *that* time of the year, the time when Uncle Ash disappeared, if only for a week or two.

The hand brake protested as Uncle Ash yanked it into place. Corolla, his plump white fox terrier, leapt out of the driver's-side door as it opened and barreled toward Bone. She scooped up the little dog and walked slowly toward the truck. The other dogs, Kiaweh and Kitty Hawk, hung their heads out of the passenger side, their tails thunking against the dash. Uncle Ash tugged at the tarp covering the bed of the truck, retying one corner. Underneath it, Bone knew he had his army-issue camping gear, fishing rods, and an extra gas can.

Bone laid her hand on the warm hood of the truck. Once again she saw Uncle Ash and the dogs driving along a long white strip of beach, their heads lolling out the windows, Uncle Ash's included, relishing the warm spray of salt water against their faces. She could feel something lifting in him, something to do with the

10

Great War, as he breathed in the sea air and wide-open spaces. Bone had discovered his little secret back around Halloween. In early December every year, he escaped to the Outer Banks or some other beach in the Carolinas. She should've known since all his dogs were named after those places.

"Where are you going this time?" Bone asked.

"As far as the gas rationing will take me." He unrolled what was left of his Lucky Strike cigarette, letting the ashes fall to the ground and grinding them out with his boot. Then he slipped the paper into his pocket. He called this fieldstripping; it was something the army had taught him in the Great War. "But I'll be back for Christmas."

A black Ford crawled by without stopping. Ruby waved, but Aunt Mattie didn't even look their way. The back seat was full of boxes.

"Are you and Mattie talking yet?" He watched his sister pull up to the parsonage.

"Are you?" She'd tried to forgive her aunt for almost drowning her, trying to baptize the Gift right out of her, but Mattie had done everything in her power to make that nigh on impossible.

Uncle Ash laughed. "That's a whole 'nuther story. Let's declare a truce for Christmas. With Mattie. With everyone." He fished the packet of Luckies out of his coat pocket. "With ourselves." He got that faraway look in his eye. Sometimes Uncle Ash disappeared without leaving. "A Christmas truce."

Bone groaned. "That's easy for you to do, seeing as you're

11

retreating to the beach." She instantly regretted it.

Uncle Ash flinched. He tossed the packet into the truck, checked the other tie-downs, and then reached across the big dogs to pull something out of the glove box.

"I didn't mean it that way," Bone said as he rounded the front of the truck and kicked a tire. He was the last person on earth Bone wanted to hurt.

"Forever Girl, did I ever tell you about the Christmas Truce of 1914?" He took out two peppermint sticks from the little paper sack in his hand and handed Bone one. Sticking a slim book in his coat pocket, he motioned for her to sit on the running board with him. She happily obliged.

"The war had been going on for six months or so. The Brits, French, and Germans were all dug in in Flanders." It was a part of Belgium, he explained. He was still in Canada at the time, training with the Expeditionary, and they didn't get to the trenches until months later. But he'd met men who'd been there that Christmas. Uncle Ash sucked on a peppermint stick for a long moment. "Our trenches were only a few hundred yards from the Germans'. In between, there was this barren ground called a no-man's-land, marked off with razor wire. On Christmas Eve, the Brits heard the Germans singing." As the church choir started up with the same hymn again, Uncle Ash paused to listen. He smiled. "They were singing this song, 'O Holy Night,' only in German. The Brits joined in. After the singing died down, one of the Jerries yelled, 'Tomorrow, we no shoot, you no shoot.'"

"Did they?" Bone bit into her peppermint stick. "Not shoot, I mean."

"Sure enough, come Christmas morning, the line was as quiet as church on Saturday night." Uncle Ash caught a white flake on his tongue. "Soldiers on both sides started popping their heads up over the trenches. Brits and Germans alike wandered out into no-man's-land. Men were soon swapping liquor and cigarettes and chocolate bars with each other. They laughed and showed each other photos of their wives and children. They sang more Christmas carols. Each side buried their dead. In some places, I heard, they even kicked a ball around."

"Was it the whole army?" She had a hard time picturing the soldiers setting aside their guns, even for Christmas.

"No," Uncle Ash said. "The brass, the generals and officers, didn't like it one bit. They even took potshots at the Jerries, trying to break the truce." He stood up and brushed off his dungarees. "And peace didn't break out again, leastwise not until November 11, 1918."

He stroked his dog tags as he talked. She'd seen them before many times. He had two silver disks tied to an old leather cord around his neck. One of the disks was a bit bigger and a different shape, an oval really. They'd seen a lot since 1914. Ash raised an eyebrow at her and quickly tucked them back into his red flannel shirt. "Remember what I said about these."

He'd told her never to touch them.

And Bone had no desire to. She didn't want to see a war that still left Uncle Ash shaken nearly twenty-five years later. "Why didn't they never have a Christmas truce again?" she asked.

Uncle Ash took a long drag on his peppermint stick and then flicked it to the ground, grinding it under his boot heel like a cigarette. "Sometimes peace takes more courage than war," he finally said. He looked up into the sky for a moment, letting a few flakes fall on his face, before buttoning up his coat. "So let's all us foot soldiers declare a truce for the season." He held out his hand to shake on it. "Including with Mattie."

"She's no foot solider." Aunt Mattie was more like those generals, always taking potshots at folks, especially Bone. Except lately, it was more like there was a no-man's-land full of razor wire between them.

"Isn't she?"

Bone shook his hand. She could hold out just fine, truce-wise, at least until Uncle Ash got back. She and Mattie would keep *not* talking to each other. That counted as a truce, right?

Uncle Ash pulled her in for a hug. "Forever Girl, I know it's hard with your daddy being Lord knows where and all. But I'll be back in plenty of time to cut us a Christmas tree and we can do up a big bonfire and tell stories . . ."

"Scary ones?" Christmas was a time of ghosts and ghost stories, Mamaw always said. It was an Old Christmas tradition.

"Of course, I'll dig up a couple new spirit dog stories." Those were Uncle Ash's favorites. "Tell you what, Forever Girl," Ash said as he pulled the book out of his pocket and handed it to her.

"While I'm gone, why don't you practice your Gift on this?" It was a book of poems by this fellow McCrae who'd been in the same regiment as Uncle Ash. He'd had her practice on this object a time or two before.

The little leather book was warm in her hand. She could see Uncle Ash sitting in the back of his truck on a windswept beach, reading the poem about Flanders. As he read, the words and the crashing waves drowned out the sound of guns pounding in his head. "Don't you need this?" Bone asked.

"If ye break faith with us who die / We shall not sleep, though poppies grow / In Flanders fields," he recited. "I know it by heart by now. Hold on." He took the book back quickly, removed some letters, and handed it to Bone again.

She grinned. The first time she'd used her Gift on the book, she'd discovered love letters from Miss Spencer tucked into the pages. Uncle Ash and her had been writing each other since she left Big Vein a couple months ago. She'd been here collecting stories for the government writers' project. Normally, she taught at the women's college in Roanoke.

Uncle Ash blushed as he stuffed the letters in his pocket. "After the war, the Belgians planted poppies to commemorate those who died there, fields and fields of red poppies." He gazed off toward the river, not quite disappearing this time.

"I'd like to see that," Bone said. Poppies were a real pretty flower. Why had no one in the family been named after that particular plant? Almost everyone in the Reed and Phillips families was named after some tree, flower, or shrub. Laurel. Willow. Ash. Acacia. Hawthorne. Even Mattie's real name was Amarantha.

"Me, too, Forever Girl." Uncle Ash patted his pockets for his pack of Luckies. "The only time Flanders was even remotely pretty was when it was covered in a thick blanket of snow." He shivered. "And it never stayed white for long."

Bone imagined the ghosts of all those soldiers rising up around this time of year to enjoy their truce, only to find folks fighting another war to end all wars in the snow above them.

"All right, dogs." Uncle Ash motioned for them to jump back in the truck. They dutifully piled into the cab, though the bigger ones usually rode in the back. Corolla staked out the driver's side.

"I promise to be back by Christmas," Uncle Ash said as he hugged Bone. "See if you can find out who sent me that book," he added, tapping its cover. Then he slid into the driver's seat, scooting the fox terrier over to the middle.

"White Christmas" played on the truck radio as Uncle Ash whipped the Chevy around and headed back down the gravel road to the river and the main road.

Bone ached to see him go, but she knew he needed to quiet the war still raging inside his head. She tucked the book into her butter-yellow sweater, the one that had been Mama's before she left too. Bone pulled the sweater tight around her again. It showed her a young Ash getting on a bus to go north, to go off to war. Mama's heart had been as low as Bone's was now.

But he came back. He always did.

2

U-BOAT STRIKES BRIT TROOP SHIP, KILLING 654, the headline screamed in capital letters across the Monday morning newspaper. Bone read the story over Mamaw's shoulder as she cleared the breakfast plates. Nurses and kids were among the dead. The same thing had happened to Uncle Henry's ship. A preacher, he'd given up his life jacket to save some soldier.

"Anything about Italy?" Bone asked. Daddy was headed there next, or at least that's what she and Uncle Junior figured. Daddy couldn't say, of course, in his last letter, only that he would be glad to see the end of the sand.

Mamaw flipped through the pages and stopped on a little story. "Says here the Royal Air Force is bombing railways in northern Italy."

"That's okay then," Bone said, relieved. She and Uncle Junior studied the maps when they listened to the war news every night. He reckoned the army might cross the Mediterranean from the deserts of North Africa to fight Mussolini in southern Italy. *How different had Uncle Ash's war been*, she wondered. Tonight she'd check the maps to see where Flanders was.

"Hard to believe this war has been going on for a whole year." Mamaw sipped her coffee, glancing up at the electric clock over the back door. "Law, is that the time? School's fixing to start and Mattie'll be waiting on me." She gulped down the rest of her coffee and headed toward the door.

Bone grabbed her sack lunch, books, and coat—and hustled to keep up. Acacia Reed did not dillydally.

Ruby was sitting on the front steps of the parsonage. She wiped her eyes as Mamaw opened the front gate. "She's been at it for hours already." Ruby sniffed. "Can't wait to get out of this hick town, she says."

Mamaw pecked Ruby on the check. "It'll all work out, honey," she told Ruby. "Radford ain't that far away."

"Might as well be France." Ruby snorted. Mamaw hugged her.

Bone leaned on the gate as Ruby gathered up her books. The parsonage, freshly painted snow white, glistened in the sun. This house and the church next door were the only truly white buildings in a "hick town" of clapboard gray and coal black. The new preacher would be moving his family in after New Year's.

"I tell you what, girls." Mamaw sat down on the step next to Ruby and motioned Bone over. "We're going to have a proper old-fashioned Christmas—plum through to Old Christmas."

Old Christmas was the day folks used to celebrate Christmas long ago. January 6. Twelfth Night. Some, like Great-grandma Daisy, had still celebrated it when Mamaw was young.

Bone loved hearing about Old Christmas. Folks believed ghosts walked the earth in the darkest part of the year and miracles happened, like talking animals and blooming elder bushes. Those were her kind of stories.

The lace curtain in the window moved, and the door cracked open.

"About time you got here, Mother," Aunt Mattie said, box in hand. Her hair was tied up in a kerchief and she wore an apron over her dress. She didn't look in Bone's direction. "Ruby, stand up, young lady! You'll ruin your dress."

Ruby obliged.

Aunt Mattie glanced at Bone, running her eyes over Bone's dungarees, boots, and coat. Then she turned back to Ruby. Aunt Mattie always looked at Bone like she was something that needed fixing. While Bone was living at the parsonage, Aunt Mattie tried fixing her, with Ruby's castoffs and rules about who she could see. Now, Aunt Mattie didn't bother. Bone wasn't sure which was worse.

Mattie fussed over Ruby's hair and smoothed out her dress. "You don't want to look a mess when Robbie Matthews asks you to the Christmas dance."

"Mother." Ruby rolled her eyes.

Bone ignored them. "Uncle Ash said we can tell ghost stories around the bonfire." The Christmas after Mama died they'd had a bonfire up on Reed Mountain, her and Mamaw and Uncle Ash. That was the first time he'd told her about spirit dogs. He told many such tales that night. In her favorite one, the dog appeared to protect a little girl whose family had been treating her awful. She couldn't see the ghost herself. The dog only showed himself to those who were mean to her. The crackling fire and the scary stories had been just what Bone needed to chase the ghosts and sadness away, if just for an hour or two. Bone sighed. Uncle Ash better get himself home by Christmas.

Mamaw stretched herself up. "Of course! And we'll make a racket to scare off any haints." She smiled at Aunt Mattie as she brushed by her into the house.

"Mother, that is wholly inappropriate!" Aunt Mattie yelled after her.

"It is not," Mamaw said. "The Yuletide is the dark part of the year, and you've got to tell spooky stories on Christmas Eve or Twelfth Night."

"That's heathen nonsense, Mother." Aunt Mattie pursed her lips.

Bone bit hers. A truce, a Christmas truce, she'd promised Uncle Ash until he returned.

The preacher's wife didn't approve of ghost stories and heathen ways at Halloween let alone Christmas. She'd even fought Uncle

Henry about putting up Christmas trees. She'd always quote some verse in Isaiah or Jeremiah about the pagans nailing up a tree. And Uncle Henry would always point out they didn't have Christmas back in those days. Then he and Ruby would chop down the biggest Virginia pine they could fit in the parsonage.

Without Uncle Henry, Aunt Mattie would probably ban Christmas trees. This Christmas was going to be tough for Ruby.

"We better get to school," Bone told her cousin.

They ran up the road, sliding into the classroom just in time for the bell.

Bone settled into her seat. It was in the open ground between where Ruby, Opal, Pearl, and Robbie sat—and where Jake and Clay hid out. Only they weren't there yet. This time last year, when the war first started, the sixth- and seventh-grade rows were fuller. Will and the Linkous twins had gone down into the mines. Several others had left for other reasons, their parents finding jobs or getting drafted or killed. Now Ruby would be moving to Radford soon.

Miss Johnson cleared her throat and started calling the roll. "Miss Albert . . ."

Ruby raised her hand.

Jake and Clay burst into the room, out of breath but with huge grins on their faces. "Sorry, Miss J." Jake handed her a note as they both made their way to their usual seats on the back row.

Miss Johnson tucked the note in her roll book. "Miss Croy?"

"Here!"

Bone tapped at her right cheek as Clay squeezed by. He had a streak of coal on his face, which he promptly wiped on his sleeve. "Wait till you hear what we were a-doing!" he whispered.

A pencil jabbed Bone in the back. Jake held out his grubby hand, the lifeline of his palm still gray with coal dust. In it sat a shiny dime. "Daddy paid us one a piece just for an hour's . . ."

"Mr. Lilly," Miss Johnson scolded.

Clay giggled, and Jake snatched his prize back.

Jake's dad was the outside man at the Big Vein mine. He was in charge of running the tipple and the mantrip, among other things. What did he have the boys doing? A dime was a lot of money. When the boys had worked at the mine earlier this year, they were handloaders. It didn't pay that much an hour. The miners only got $1.25 per carload. Bone wondered about that all through history, geography, and spelling.

❧

At lunch, Jake and Clay finally got to spill the beans.

"It's a regular mystery!" Jake exclaimed as he laid out his lunch. A fried bologna sandwich wrapped in creased waxed paper. An apple. And a jelly jar of rice pudding. He handed the apple to Clay without remarking on it. "Daddy got me up at the crack of dark. Then we fetched Clay." Mr. Whitaker was already at work, he explained.

"He's been at the mill since the accident," Clay said between mouthfuls of ham biscuit. His father had gotten hurt when a mine shaft had caved in on him and the Linkous twins. Marvin Linkous escaped with a scratch. Garvin's broken arm was healing fine, but Mr. Whitaker now walked with a limp. The mill was owned by the mine. Before the war, a dozen people chopped down trees and milled lumber for the mine. Now it was just Mr. Whitaker.

Bone unwrapped her drumstick as she listened to the boys.

"Daddy said he had a special job for us." Jake bit into the neatly trimmed sandwich with not a hint of crust.

"Someone's been leaving a mess of coal under the tipple every Saturday night," Clay added. The tipple loaded the coal onto the trains. And everyone knew the 8:15 was the last train. "For the past month or so."

"Mr. Matthews asked Daddy to get us in to clean it up."

"The big man asked for us by name!"

Bone shushed Clay and nodded toward the tree. Robbie Matthews was leaning against it, peeling an orange, pretending not to listen, at least until his father's name was mentioned. He tossed a rind on the ground and came toward them. He shook his head woefully before popping a juicy section of orange into his mouth.

Bone inhaled the scent of Christmas morning. The only time she got oranges was in her stocking. Daddy made sure she got one every year, no matter how broke they were.

"Father would've asked one of the n—" He stopped himself. "One of the Negroes to do it. But he thinks they're responsible."

Bone bristled at what Robbie almost said. Clay and Jake glared at Robbie, too. She couldn't tell if they were mad for the same reason she was.

"That's stupid," Bone said to Robbie. "Why in the world would Mr. Sherman or Mr. Fears be leaving coal under the tipple?" They both worked the night shift, and Tiny Sherman had just been promoted to outside man. He ran the tipple at night.

"Because, you dolt, they're stealing it—and not clever enough to clean up after themselves." Robbie spat orange pulp onto the ground.

Bone went off oranges then and there.

"Now hold on." Jake wagged a finger at Robbie. "Don't you be calling Bone names."

"And no one said anything about Tiny or Oscar being involved," Clay added.

"I heard Father say that the Sherman boy wasn't to be trusted." Robbie shrugged, looking pleased with himself.

Tiny Sherman was no boy. He was a very nice man, about Daddy's age, who'd pitched for the Negro Leagues back in the day. Mama had healed his arm when a bunch of white boys jumped him years ago, right before he was supposed to go off to play ball in Memphis. Bone's Gift had told her that. Now he worked the mines and pitched for the Big Vein team.

"Mr. Sherman is too trustworthy!" Bone shook a drumstick at Robbie Matthews.

"You would say that. Him and your Uncle Ash are pals."

"So what?" Bone bit into the chicken leg. It was true. Uncle Ash and Mr. Sherman went fishing together. And Uncle Ash treated all the animals over in Sherman's Forest, the black community just down the road. Most people liked Uncle Ash—and Tiny.

"Well, everyone knows your uncle ain't right ever since the Great War." Robbie leaned in. "That's what Daddy says anyways."

Chewing furiously, Bone slapped the drumstick against the wax paper and stood up. No one bad-mouthed her Uncle Ash, even if they might be right. She could feel Jake and Clay rise beside her. "Just shut up," she spat out.

"Who knows? Maybe they're in on this thing together." Robbie smirked. The smirk suddenly turned to a smile as Ruby walked up with Opal and Pearl—the Little Jewels. He'd always been sweet on Ruby, walking her and her friends everywhere, hanging on her every word. Only now she was leaving, and he seemed more determined—and spiteful—than ever. Bone didn't understand either.

"What's this?" Ruby asked, glaring at Robbie.

"Oh, nothing!" He whispered something in her ear and then said so everyone could hear, "Let's go eat inside where it's more civilized." He took Ruby by the arm, and she reluctantly followed with Opal and Pearl in tow. Robbie shot a look at Bone that clearly said this was not over.

"Aw, forget him!" Jake said loudly as he plopped back down on the bench to finish his lunch.

"Yeah!" Clay followed suit. "How 'bout a story, Bone?"

"A scary one," Jake added. "Granddaddy says Christmas is really a time for ghost stories and such, since it comes at the darkest part of the year. They scare off the haints and bad luck."

Bone sighed and sank back down onto her seat. The chicken didn't look so appealing anymore. She tore open a biscuit and slathered it with apple butter. Why would Mr. Matthews or Robbie say those things about Tiny—or Uncle Ash, for that matter? She wished Uncle Ash hadn't left already. He'd only been gone two days but it felt like two weeks.

"Bone?" Jake prodded her.

"How about a ghost dog story?" she asked, finally. They were Uncle Ash's favorite. He always said ghost or spirit or devil dogs could be an omen of death or a bringer of justice—or both. She scratched her head for one she hadn't told the boys yet. "Y'all have heard of Swift's Silver Mine, right?"

Heads nodded eagerly. Jake beckoned over the rest of the kids eating outside. "Bone's getting ready to tell a good one." Half the upper classes huddled around Bone's table.

"Yes, that Swift fellow discovered a mother lode of silver in the mountains," Clay said.

"Before the Revolution . . ."

"In Virginia . . ."

"No, Granddaddy said Tennessee."

"Kentucky!" another voice threw in.

"Okay, okay." Bone beckoned them to settle down around her. "Y'all are right. Nobody knows where that mine was—and Swift went blind and could never find it himself again. But there was this woman who thought she'd found it once. Her and her husband was searching through the hills. She saw this black dog, as big as a yearling, with eyes the size of saucers standing guard over the entrance of a cave."

"A ghost dog?"

"Yep. The woman tried to get closer—and the dog stood his ground, eyes swirling at her—so she ran off to get her husband. As soon as she looked over her shoulder—that dog disappeared into thin air!"

"Did they find the mine?"

"Nope, they never could find that place—or the ghost dog— again," Bone concluded.

Miss Johnson rang the bell, calling an end to lunch.

⁓

Back inside, everyone was talking and some were still eating. Miss Johnson usually allowed them a few minutes to wash up and visit the johnny house before she started class back up.

"Did I ever tell you Uncle Ash thought he saw a devil dog

during the war?" Bone asked Jake and Clay as they slid into their seats at the back of the classroom.

"No!" The boys scooted their desks closer.

"He was in the trenches, and this big black dog started walking across no-man's-land toward him and his dogs. Uncle Ash ran the messenger dogs for his battalion. He thought he was done for, and the ghost dog was there to tell him a mortar shell or gas attack was about to get him." Bone paused for effect.

"Well?"

"Turns out it was one of the Germans' dogs that had gotten lost."

The boys groaned.

"He patched it up and sent it back to their lines."

Robbie Matthews snorted. "My daddy was a *real* hero in the Great War," he told Ruby loud enough for everyone to hear. "He's got a box of souvenirs to prove it."

"Nuts to him," Jake replied.

Miss Johnson cleared her throat and started lecturing about Charles Dickens.

"Did your uncle ever see a real ghost dog?" Clay whispered.

Bone nodded.

Uncle Ash had seen a ghost dog outside Aunt Mattie's house the day Mama died there.

It was probably a good thing that lady didn't see that ghost dog guarding Swift's Mine ever again.

BONE HAD ALREADY READ several of Mr. Dickens's books, including the one Miss Johnson was assigning to the seventh graders. It was her favorite seeing as it was a Christmas ghost story. "Christmas almost died out as a holiday on both sides of the Atlantic—until *A Christmas Carol* came along," Miss Johnson told the class. "Well, Dickens's story wasn't the only thing—"

The mine whistle blew.

It hadn't done so since October when Mr. Whitaker and one of the Linkous twins got trapped after a shaft collapsed. Will had single-handedly rescued Garvin Linkous.

Jake put a hand on Clay's shoulder as they stood. Both of their daddies were safe, working outside the mine.

Bone and Ruby exchanged a glance. Uncle Junior and Will were still down in Big Vein.

Miss Johnson opened the classroom door. "Take your coats!" she called as Bone and Ruby scooted out, followed by the boys and the Little Jewels. Everyone had someone at the mine. Bone pulled her mother's butter-yellow sweater tight around her as she ran. Woven in the very fabric of the yarn, she could see every time Mama had sprinted over this same ground, panicked that something had happened to Daddy, Junior, or Papaw.

As usual when the whistle blew, the whole community turned up outside the mine entrance. The wind whipped through the hollow, and a tiny speck of snow fell. Bone and Ruby found Mamaw who'd run down from the parsonage. Alone. Jake and Clay ran to their fathers, both of them working up top. Mr. Whitaker limped over to the mine entrance, and Mr. Lilly threw the mantrip in gear. He exchanged a few words with the boys.

Jake came tearing back toward Bone. "Daddy says they don't know nothing. Garvin rang up to tell them to pull the whistle—and call the sheriff," he panted.

A murmur went through the crowd around them.

"Sheriff?" Mamaw said to Mrs. Price. "They never done that before."

The mantrip emerged from the mine entrance with a rattle. One by one, men covered with coal dust and ash peeled themselves out of the little tram. A tall wiry man, who could only be Uncle Junior, unfolded himself and rounded the back of the trip.

Another dusty form, almost as tall, met him there. Will.

Mamaw let out a breath—and so did Bone. And Ruby.

Uncle Junior spoke to Mr. Whitaker, who then hobbled around with a clipboard calling out names: Albert Price! Marvin Linkous! Garvin Linkous! Will Kincaid! He ticked off the names of everyone on day shift—which wasn't that many anymore.

A murmur went around the crowd again.

Everyone seemed to be there. Instead of heading toward their families, the men walled off Junior and Will as they emerged from the back of the trip carrying something—or someone—covered by a tarp. They laid it gently on the cold ground.

Uncle Junior took the clipboard—and flipped through it. With a shake of his head, he handed it back to Mr. Whitaker.

Slowly, the men of Big Vein's day shift drifted toward their families and loved ones.

"Must be someone from the night shift," Mamaw murmured.

Uncle Junior stood there dazed for a moment, wiping the back of his hand across his forehead. Then he saw Mamaw, Bone, and Ruby. He pulled the brim of his cap down tight, his face still streaked with sweat and coal dust, and walked across the gravel to them.

"Who is it?" Mamaw asked gently. She took the kerchief from her hair and handed it to Junior.

"Danged if I know!" He wiped at his face, making it more gray than anything. "And I should know!" He scanned the crowd. "Everyone, day and night shift, is accounted for." Uncle Junior was the day shift supervisor now that Daddy had been drafted.

"Could the night shift have missed someone?" Mamaw asked. She stuffed the blackened kerchief into her pocket.

"They checked off everyone on the list." Uncle Junior put his mining hat back on. "Besides, that was Saturday night. Someone would have noticed anyone missing come Sunday."

"What'd he look like?" Bone asked. Everybody knew everybody around Big Vein, even if they didn't work in the mine anymore.

"That's the thing." Uncle Junior avoided looking at Bone. "It's kind of hard to tell. The body was covered in debris. A beam must've . . ."

"Oh," Mamaw said quietly.

Bone didn't get it, but she let it go.

"Maybe he's indigent," Aunt Mattie said, suddenly appearing at his shoulder. She'd taken her sweet time coming down to the mine. No longer in a kerchief, her hair was neatly done, and she'd shed her apron. "Remember the man Daddy found?" she asked her brother.

Uncle Junior nodded. "The fellow died in his sleep. Didn't know the ventilation wasn't running."

Bone did understand this. Men used to come looking for work all the time during the Depression. Daddy would invite them home. Mama—and later Mrs. Price—would feed them a good meal for the price of a story and send them on their way.

Sometimes they'd sneak into the mine if the weather was bad. The Superior Anthracite Company didn't pay to have the fans running when the miners weren't mining. A man could suffocate, Daddy always said, if the air wasn't circulating.

"We haven't found one like that in years, but you never know." Junior walked back to Mr. Whitaker and checked the clipboard one more time. They fell into a heated discussion.

While Junior and the other miners debated who it could be, Mr. Matthews pulled up in his Cadillac. He parked it in front of the store.

"That's new, too," Mamaw remarked.

Bone didn't recall seeing him at the accident in September.

"If it's a bum, Robinson Matthews will want them to get right back to work," Mattie said to no one in particular.

Mamaw gave her the stink eye.

Mr. Matthews was taking his sweet time. He was still in his Cadillac.

⁘

Next, the sheriff's car parted the crowd and parked right by the mine entrance. Sheriff Alfred Taylor hopped out and shooed everyone away from the body. Uncle Junior quickly filled him in and showed him the clipboard, listing the names of who it wasn't.

Mr. Matthews muscled his way through the crowd and collared Uncle Junior. He stiffened as his boss laid into him. Bone could only hear a few words. *Bum. Army. Quota.*

Aunt Mattie looked smug.

Christmas truce, Bone reminded herself. *At least until Uncle Ash gets back.*

Mr. Matthews stomped off to lay into Mr. Lilly next.

The sheriff knelt down. His face went white as he pulled up the tarp. Dropping it, he turned his head away for a moment. Then taking a deep breath, he lifted the tarp again. Bone understood now why they couldn't tell who it was. A beam must've crushed the man's face. This time the sheriff felt around the man's body.

"Of course, he's looking for the man's wallet," Bone whispered to Ruby. She'd seen that in detective movies.

The sheriff tugged at something before carefully laying the tarp back across the body. He peered at the thing—and then gave it to Uncle Junior.

Sun glinted off the silver disk in his hand, a bit of leather cord dangling free.

A dog tag? The men who'd ridden the rails looking for work had often been veterans, Bone told herself. *Lots of men wore dog tags.*

Junior stared at the tag for the longest time—before dropping to his knees like someone had shot him.

4

MAMAW WAS AT UNCLE JUNIOR'S SIDE before Bone could even blink.

The dog tag on a leather cord.

Uncle Junior on his knees.

She ran. The open ground between her and Uncle Junior and Mamaw yawned before Bone. The more she ran, the farther away they seemed to get.

Will snagged her just before she reached them—and the body. She thrashed against his wiry arms.

"You don't wanna see this," he whispered.

Bone thrashed again and then surrendered. Will held her as they stood a few feet from the covered body.

Mamaw rounded it and knelt beside Uncle Junior. She

pulled up the tarp, holding it so Bone couldn't see what they were seeing. Mamaw flinched and looked away. With a deep breath, she steeled herself to look again. "It ain't him." She lay the tarp over the man and tucked the edges under him.

"That's the only identification on him." The sheriff pointed to the tag still in Uncle Junior's hand. He gently pried Uncle Junior's fingers open, revealing a tarnished round tag with Sgt Ash Reed stamped into it.

"No!" Bone yelped. It was the same dog tag she'd seen often around Uncle Ash's neck—and it had his name on it. Will held her tight. He smelled like sweat and dirt and sorrow.

"Will." Uncle Junior looked up. "Take Bone home." He glanced toward the crowd. "Ruby, too."

Bone didn't, couldn't budge.

"It ain't him." Mamaw was adamant. "Don't you think I know my own son?"

"Mama." Junior pulled himself to his feet, ignoring the sheriff's outstretched hand. Gently, he laid the dog tag in Mamaw's palm.

She let it fall through her fingers.

"It's just a bum, Al." Mr. Matthews pushed in, yelling at the sheriff. "My people need to get back to work. The war effort won't wait."

"It's gonna have to." The sheriff picked the dog tag up from the dirt and showed the inscription to Mr. Matthews.

"What the Sam Hill—" he sputtered, backing away.

"Ash Reed?" So many thoughts had gone across that man's face in those few seconds, but Bone couldn't figure what nary a one of them might have been.

He cleared his throat. "Junior, I'm sorry. Of course, Sheriff, you do what you need to do." Mr. Matthews motioned for everyone to go home. No one did. So he just kind of faded back through the crowd, and moments later the Cadillac peeled down the mine road.

"It can't be him," Bone pleaded.

"Will, please take her home," Uncle Junior said once again, his voice breaking. He caught Bone's eye and nodded ever so slightly.

Her knees melted. It was Uncle Ash.

She let Will lead her away. Slowly. Her world had collapsed upon her, the weight of it all making it hard to breathe, let alone walk.

"It isn't him," Mamaw hollered after her.

"Mama," Junior said. "The tag has his name on it."

"I know my own son—and you should know your brother. That ain't him!" Mamaw was still adamant.

Bone's legs solidified under her—and she shrugged off Will's arm.

She could breathe again. If Mamaw was sure, then it couldn't be Uncle Ash. It couldn't be.

The sheriff said something that Bone couldn't hear. And she didn't want to look back.

They walked down the gravel road toward the boardinghouse. The bare tree branches scraped against each other as a breeze passed over the woods on the side of the road. The 2:25 chugged along the river in the distance. And the only other sound was that of patent leather shoes running after them.

"Is it true?" Ruby gasped as she caught up.

Bone shook her head and dashed up to the boardinghouse where she'd lived with Daddy since Mama died. She sunk onto the steps. She'd thought about Daddy dying in the war. He was probably in Italy by now, fighting Nazis and fascists. But Uncle Ash? He'd survived the Great War, fighting in the trenches for longer than most Americans, and even been buried alive in a collapsed tunnel for days. This made no kind of sense. She'd never known Uncle Ash to go near the mines. He'd gone all white and shaky that time she'd just talked about what she saw when she touched Will Kincaid's dinner bucket. Will's father had died down in Big Vein—a lot like that fellow under the tarp. Bone had felt the blackness fall on him.

Uncle Ash lived through that blackness for days. He'd never go into the mine.

Will sat down next to her.

"Is it?" Ruby looked from Bone to Will.

"The dog tag says Sgt Ash Reed," Will whispered.

"Oh, Bone!" Ruby collapsed next to Bone. "Not Uncle Ash, too."

Bone put an arm around her cousin. "It's not him." Bone

dried her tears on the sleeve of her butter-yellow sweater. She caught a glimpse of a younger Uncle Ash decked out in bank clothes dragging behind Uncle Junior and Papaw. Toward the mine. That couldn't be right. Maybe the memory was from before the war.

It was not Uncle Ash under that tarp.

5

THE LITTLE BELL OVER the boardinghouse's front door jangled as it opened and closed well into the evening. Dishes clattered onto the kitchen table. Voices murmured sympathy. With death, folks bring pecan pies, green bean casserole, and ham biscuits. They also bring pounds of sugar and pinto beans and coffee and such to get the family through their loss. Bone listened to it all as she stared at the spidery cracks in her bedroom ceiling, *In Flanders Fields and Other Poems* lying by her side.

It wasn't Uncle Ash. And why were folks bringing covered dishes to the boardinghouse? He didn't live here. Uncle Junior did. She did. Uncle Ash lived up on Reed Mountain with Mamaw, who was, last Bone had seen her, stewing in the kitchen, muttering about needing to get home. Usually it was Uncle Ash who drove her.

Bone sat up in bed.

Where was his truck? And the dogs? If that was him—which it wasn't, mind you—those dogs would be right there with him, wherever he went.

She pulled Uncle Ash's book up to her face and breathed in the pages. They smelled of peppermint and tobacco and motor oil, all the things he kept in his glove box. The waves crashed on the beach late at night, fish crackled over a fire, and the dogs snored softly beside Uncle Ash as he read under a starstruck sky. That's where he was right now, sitting on the sands of Ocracoke or Hatteras.

And he wouldn't go down in that mine anyways.

Would he? She stroked the sleeve of the butter-yellow sweater again. *Did Uncle Ash go into the mines?* The sweater showed her the same scene, a young Uncle Ash tagging along behind his brother and daddy. Mama wasn't any help. That didn't prove anything.

It wasn't him.

The house was finally quiet.

Bone peeled herself off the bed, tucked the book under her arm, and crept down the back stairs.

In the kitchen, Mrs. Price scrubbed at the sink with a fury. Ruby was opening and closing up cabinets. The table was full of covered dishes and a few pounding boxes. Ruby grabbed a tin of crackers from the closest box and shoved it into a crammed cabinet.

"Bone!" Ruby hugged her. "Please eat something. There's an awful lot of food." She took a ham biscuit from a plate on the table and placed it in Bone's hand. "Eat." Ruby tore off a piece of biscuit for herself.

Bone put it in her mouth and chewed. It tasted like sawdust. She kept chewing so she didn't need to talk.

"Mother Reed and your mother can take a bunch of this," Mrs. Price told Ruby as she surveyed the table. Her hands were raw from cleaning, and the normally spic-and-span kitchen downright sparkled. "Honey, have some milk, too." She directed that at Bone.

She kept chewing—and peeked into the parlor.

Uncle Junior sat slumped in his chair, staring at the fire. Through the front window, Bone could see Will on the porch swing.

"Where's Mamaw?" Bone asked Ruby.

"Mother ran her home." Ruby stuffed a preacher cookie in her mouth. "Mamaw is plum losing her mind."

Mrs. Price clanked a dish down on the counter. "She's just being a mother. Your children, no matter how old they are, aren't supposed to die before you. First, Willow—" She cut herself off.

Bone knew what she was going to say. First Bone's mother and now Uncle Ash.

And Mamaw had soft spots for Mama and Ash. Yes, she loved all her children, but these two both had the strong Gifts, Mamaw had told Bone, just like her and Bone. Mrs. Price didn't know about that part. Folks outside the family didn't know about the Gifts. People just assumed Uncle Ash had a way with animals, Mama was a natural nurse, and Mamaw had learned everything from her mother. At least all of their Gifts were useful.

"Well, it's hard to accept, especially if it comes sudden." Mrs. Price wiped her eyes on her apron. One of her boys, Bone suddenly remembered, had died in the last war.

Death was always hard to accept, Bone thought. But this wasn't right. It wasn't Uncle Ash. It couldn't be. Bone bit into the cookie Ruby offered her. It tasted like ashes, sickly sweet ashes.

⁂

A rap came from the back door. Mrs. Price ushered in Mr. Sherman and his Aunt Queenie.

Bone tucked Uncle Ash's book into her back pocket.

"Come here, child." She crossed the kitchen and wrapped Bone in a hug. Ruby stepped back, but Queenie reached for her, too, folding her and Bone both into her strong arms.

Mr. Sherman clutched his Sunday hat in front of him. Most days he wore his Memphis Red Sox cap, even at the mine. "Miss

Bone, I'm real sorry about Ash." The words caught in his throat. "He was a good 'un, just like your mama."

The sweater showed Bone a much younger Tiny and Ash sitting on Queenie's porch. Mama carefully stitched a cut over Tiny's eye as Ash held a cloth to his own bleeding lip. They weren't much older than Will. Tiny winced as Mama snipped the end of the catgut. Ash elbowed him. "*Them Matthews boys look worse than us,*" he said with a stupid grin on his face. Mama glared at him. "*They jumped us.*" Ash pouted. Bone cracked a teeny, tiny smile.

"Junior here?" Mr. Sherman asked.

"In the parlor," Mrs. Price answered. "Why don't you all go in and I'll fetch some coffee." She nodded toward Ruby. "And a bite to eat."

Ruby sprang into action, obviously relieved to make herself useful.

Aunt Queenie fussed about them making a fuss.

"No, I need something to do, and I'm sure Junior will want to talk to you. And Mother Reed'll be back soon."

"Mother took her home to get some things," Ruby explained as she laid out some cookies on a chipped plate. Mrs. Price swapped the damaged one out for a clean one from the dish rack.

～⁓

In the parlor, Junior stirred himself and stood to shake Tiny Sherman's hand. He motioned for them all to sit down.

Will appeared from the front porch and nodded to the Shermans. The three men played on the mine baseball team together. Tiny pitched, Junior caught, and Will played shortstop. But, as Robbie Matthews pointed out, it was Tiny and Uncle Ash who were the real friends.

Mr. Sherman explained how the sheriff had stopped the night shift at the change house and made them go home. "It was a crime scene, he said." Tiny shook his head. "Mr. Matthews was fuming about the quota."

"Bet he was," Junior said flatly.

"Was the body really found down in the mine?" Mr. Sherman asked Uncle Junior.

The body. Mr. Sherman didn't say it was Uncle Ash.

Junior nodded. "Will found him."

A bolt went through Bone. She hadn't thought about who'd actually run across the body. Poor Will. She motioned for him to come sit beside her on the hearth.

"Shaft twenty-seven." Will didn't move.

"That's real peculiar," Tiny said after a moment. "Twenty-seven, you say?"

Will nodded. "Under a beam. Covered with lime."

Tiny cocked his head. "Lime?"

Mrs. Price swept into the parlor and set down a tray on the coffee table.

"This whole thing makes no sense." Junior took a cup of coffee from Mrs. Price.

She handed everyone else except Bone a cup. Ruby offered up the chocolate chip cookies. Nobody was much hungry.

"Oscar and his crew was down in twenty-seven Saturday night taking out beams so y'all could use them for the new branch," Tiny explained. Even with the mill running, the mine never had enough timber to brace the shafts. So the miners often took them out of old shafts, like twenty-seven. "Never saw nothing—or no one—who shouldn't be there."

Junior took a long sip of his coffee.

"It's mighty peculiar. Your brother never would go down there." Mr. Sherman leaned in. "Leastwise not of his own accord," he added in a hushed voice.

Junior nodded slowly. "I've been thinking just that . . ."

Bone shot a look at Will. Uncle Ash would never have gone down in the mine—unless someone made him. Or worse. "Do you mean someone dragged—," Bone started to ask.

"Where's Acacia at?" Aunt Queenie interrupted. Ruby had told her, but Queenie was eyeing first Uncle Junior and Mr. Sherman and then Bone and Ruby. The menfolk took the hint, both turning their full attention to their coffee.

Bone crossed her arms and stared at Queenie. She hated when the grown-ups decided something wasn't fit for twelve-year-olds to hear.

Queenie and Mamaw were friends—and professional colleagues, as Mamaw liked to say. Aunt Queenie birthed babies and saw to children and women in Sherman's Forest. Mother

Reed supplied the herbal teas, salves, and tinctures.

"Mama said something about proof and made Mattie drive her back up the mountain." With a glance at the clock on the mantel, Uncle Junior got up and turned the radio on low. "Mind if we listen to the war news?"

Nobody objected. Everyone had somebody over there—or soon would. Aunt Queenie's youngest was in a tank battalion training at some camp in Louisiana.

"She doesn't think it's Ash," Bone whispered.

"She would know, wouldn't she?" Queenie whispered back.

Everyone else had insisted Mamaw was wrong. "Thank you," Bone mouthed.

                                     ~

When the war news came on the radio, Uncle Junior handed Bone their map from the mantel. Reluctantly she rolled it out on the floor in front of the fire. The Brits began raiding ships in the French port of Bordeaux. A U-boat sunk off Greenland. Another U-boat torpedoed a British ocean liner west of the Azores. Bone found them off the coast of Portugal. And the Germans in North Africa were continuing to withdraw west toward Tunisia.

"Where's Flanders?" she asked Uncle Junior.

He didn't answer.

The screen door flew open, and the unmistakable sound of Mamaw's boots tromped across the kitchen.

"Mother, you've got to listen to reason," Aunt Mattie's voice trailed after her.

"I will when I hear some." Mamaw strode into the parlor waving a blue flannel shirt.

Uncle Ash's.

"That poor man we saw today was wearing one like this." She threw it at Uncle Junior. Mamaw crossed her arms and stared at Junior like he was supposed to get it.

The shirt wafted to the floor across Bone's map.

She scooped up the shirt and hugged it to her. It smelled of tobacco, peppermint sticks, Ivory soap, dogs, and a whiff of something else. It was Uncle Ash's shirt, no doubt. She saw a flash of him cleaning a stone out of a bay gelding's hoof.

"Your brother only has one of them this color—and it's right there."

Uncle Junior rose to his feet.

"Oh Mother," Aunt Mattie clucked. "Surely, Ash has got more than one blue shirt. Maybe he bought himself another on one of his *little trips*."

The way she said "little trips" got Bone's dander up. *Truce. A Christmas truce, at least until Uncle Ash got back.* And he would be back.

Mamaw wheeled around on her daughter. "Honestly, Mattie, who do you think washes and sews your brother's clothes?" She had evidently not declared a cease-fire.

Mr. Sherman and Aunt Queenie rose from the settee.

"Mother, Junior has . . . guests." Aunt Mattie stumbled over the last words.

"I'm not blind, Amarantha," Mamaw said. "Or crazy." She hugged Queenie. "Ester, I'm glad you're here; you, too, Tiny."

"Acacia, what can we do—"

Aunt Queenie was cut off by a loud insistent knock at the front door.

"Law, who could that be?" Mrs. Price hurried to answer. Folk usually just walked into the boardinghouse, the front of it at least.

"Might be the man from the funeral parlor," Aunt Mattie said. "I called him this afternoon."

"You did not!" Mamaw whirled on Mattie. "Who gave you the right?"

Bone leapt to her feet and stood beside Mamaw. How dare Aunt Mattie start planning the funeral—without Mamaw and without even knowing if it was Uncle Ash. Which it wasn't!

"Mama, let me do this for him," Aunt Mattie said quietly.

All the fire went out of Mamaw as she took Aunt Mattie's hand.

Bone crossed her arms. Aunt Mattie had never been nice to Uncle Ash that she could remember. Why was she starting now? Why was she in such an all-fired hurry to bury him? Even if it wasn't him. Which it wasn't.

"Maybe we best go," Mr. Sherman said to his aunt. She nodded, and they headed toward the kitchen.

The back door creaked open.

Sheriff Taylor strode into the parlor from the front hall just as a deputy appeared from the kitchen, blocking the Shermans from leaving. The county only had two lawmen, and they had Aunt Queenie and Tiny boxed in.

"Oscar said you'd be here, Tiny." The sheriff nodded to the deputy. "Raymond Arthur Sherman, I'm arresting you for the murder of Ash Reed."

The deputy stepped forward and clapped handcuffs around Tiny's wrists.

Bone dropped Uncle Ash's shirt to the floor.

<hr>

"It's not him," Bone broke the silence in the wake of Tiny Sherman's exit in handcuffs. She meant both Uncle Ash and Mr. Sherman. Mamaw shushed her.

The sheriff ignored her anyway.

"Queenie, you need to come with me," he said. "Now."

Aunt Queenie took a deep breath and forced it out like she was calming a mighty storm raging inside herself. Mamaw reached out a hand, but Aunt Queenie brushed it away. Bone saw the sad fury in her eyes.

Uncle Junior stepped between them and the sheriff. "Al, we've all known Tiny since we was kids. He's a decent, hardworking man."

"Don't mix in this, Junior." The sheriff leaned in. "It'll only make it harder on him."

Junior stiffened. He exchanged a glance with Mamaw, who shook her head a tiny bit.

Queenie tugged her blouse straight, tucked her handbag under her arm, and stuck her chin out as she walked past Uncle Junior and the sheriff and out the front door. "You coming, Mr. Al?"

Like most folks of a certain age around Big Vein, Bone thought, Mr. Taylor had probably been brought into the world by Queenie Sherman. Yet she still had to call him Mr.

"Make sure nothing happens to either of them, Al," Uncle Junior told the sheriff before he turned and followed Aunt Queenie to his car.

A cold chill ran through Bone.

"Certain people," Uncle Junior explained as they watched the sheriff's taillights fade into the darkness, "might get it into their heads to take justice into their own hands."

Certain *white* people.

Bone pulled the butter-yellow sweater tight around her. She saw Mama mending a younger Tiny's shattered pitching arm. Certain white people weren't motivated by justice.

6

BACK IN THE PARLOR, Uncle Junior turned off the radio and rammed a poker into the fire. Sparks flew and the embers crackled. He braced himself against the mantel and stared into the flames.

Aunt Mattie perched herself on the settee and poured a cup of cold coffee. Mamaw paced behind her.

The silence was quickly unbearable, and Bone had so many questions.

Mrs. Price maneuvered Ruby toward the kitchen. "Bone, come help us clean up."

Bone stood her ground in the middle of the parlor. "What will happen to Mr. Sherman?" she asked.

Aunt Mattie set her cup down with a clatter. "We've

got more pressing matters to discuss, young lady."

"Amarantha," Uncle Junior warned before dropping into his chair.

"More pressing than an innocent black man accused of a murder?" Mamaw snapped. "That fellow over in Wytheville was dragged out of his cell and lynched by a mob!"

Could that happen to Tiny Sherman? Bone looked to Uncle Junior for reassurance. He didn't meet her eye.

"Mother, that was nearly twenty years ago," Mattie replied.

Uncle Junior snorted.

Aunt Mattie glared at him. "This is 1942. The citizens of this county are not going to take justice into their own hands."

Bone sank into the seat by the hearth. She knew some whites still hated folks like Mr. Sherman and Aunt Queenie on account of their skin color. But would they go so far as to break him out of jail and murder him?

"Mama, I know you don't want to hear this, but we got to make some funeral arrangements for Ash." Aunt Mattie tried to catch Mamaw's hand and gently guide her to the settee.

Mamaw wasn't having it. She rounded the couch and sat by Bone on the hearth.

"It's not him," Bone repeated, on the verge of tears. Mamaw took Bone's hand.

"Oh, for the love of Pete, Mother!" Aunt Mattie went off. "You've got Laurel believing more of your nonsense. Like always."

Truce. Uncle Ash will be back.

54

"Amarantha," Junior said more sharply this time. "Now is not the time."

Bone and Mamaw turned toward him. He'd sagged back into his armchair by the fire.

"You know it's him, Junior!" Aunt Mattie demanded. "Who else would be wearing his dog tags?"

Uncle Junior stirred the fire once more and then knocked the poker against the firedogs before he spoke. "I don't know what to think. That's his dog tag, sure enough. But I know just as sure Ash wouldn't have gone down in that mine *willingly*."

Mamaw nodded.

"No, he's always running away from his responsibilities," Aunt Mattie muttered.

Truce.

"Not this again," Mamaw muttered back.

"Mattie." Uncle Junior held up a weary hand. "You remember when Ash got back from the war? Daddy got him a job in the mine with us. That first morning, he was trailing behind us. I should've known something was wrong. We didn't have the mantrip then, just mules to haul up the cars of coal. So we had to walk down the main shaft in the pitch dark. By the time we got to the cut, Ash was white as snow and shaking like a leaf in a hurricane. 'I can't do this, Daddy' was all he said before he bolted to the surface. He hadn't told neither of us about what happened in the war."

Bone sat on the hearth, relieved. That scene the sweater

showed her came after the war, but she hadn't seen the whole story. Only what Mama had witnessed. That was the problem with some objects, Bone realized. They only saw pieces of a person's story.

Aunt Mattie harrumphed.

"What did happen?" Ruby asked. She'd quietly snuck back in from the kitchen.

"He used the war as an excuse for everything!"

"Now, Mattie," Junior warned.

"No. He could've done an honest day's work just like you and Daddy. Instead he runs around playing at being a vet—"

An excuse? Running away from responsibility? Playing?

The truce was off.

"I'll tell you what happened!" Bone leapt up. "Uncle Ash got buried in a collapsed tunnel during a big battle in Belgium. For three days!" She remembered the darkness, the guns and mortars pounding the dirt above his head. She slid the poetry book out of her back pocket and wagged it in Aunt Mattie's face. "And he goes to the Outer Banks, and other beaches, this time a year because it's the wide-openest, peacefulest place he can find to quiet those guns in his head."

Aunt Mattie's mouth opened and closed shut without making a sound.

Mamaw and Uncle Junior exchanged a look. They hadn't known where Ash went.

"So Uncle Ash would've never gone into that mine!" Bone

concluded. She felt bad for betraying his secret—and breaking the truce—but darned if she was going to let Aunt Mattie talk thataway about Uncle Ash anymore.

"Exactly. Not my brother." Junior leaned back in the chair.

"That man was not Ash." Mamaw glared Aunt Mattie into keeping silent.

"So he's not dead?" Ruby said hopefully.

Uncle Junior shook his head. "I said he wouldn't go *willingly*."

Bone sank back onto the hearth, crushed under the weight of that one word. *Willingly.* Somebody could've dragged Uncle Ash down into the mine . . . after he was dead. That's what Uncle Junior meant.

No, it still wasn't him. It couldn't be. But . . .

The book in her hand was silent.

"It's still not him."

"This is all wishful thinking." Aunt Mattie guided Ruby gently toward the door. "We need to head home. Mother, you're welcome to come stay with us."

Mamaw nodded. "I'll be over directly." She squeezed Junior's arm and hugged Bone. "Thanks, Forever Girl," she whispered.

Bone ached. Only Uncle Ash called her that. It was on account of a Cherokee folk story they both loved, Forever Boy. He didn't want to grow, didn't want to face his responsibilities, so he ran away to live with the Little People in the forest. Shirking responsibilities. Running away. Did Aunt Mattie think Uncle Ash was like Forever Boy?

More loudly, Mamaw added, "He better enjoy that peace and quiet wherever he is now, 'cause I'm going to tan his backside when he gets home."

Mamaw would. And when he got home, the sheriff would have to let Mr. Sherman go, too.

Uncle Junior picked up the map and studied it for a moment. "It's right here, Bone." He placed his finger, his nail beds a permanent coal-ash gray, on northern Belgium.

FLANDERS, it said.

"Could they really hurt Mr. Sherman?" Bone asked.

Junior sighed and nodded.

7

MORNING WAS A PINPRICK OF LIGHT in the darkness. The weight of all that coal and dirt she'd dreamt of pinned her body flat to her bed. Bone felt sad when Uncle Henry died—and when Daddy left for war. She didn't remember how she felt when Mama died seeing as she was only six at the time. That was so long ago. Now, she weighed a thousand pounds. Her body acted like Uncle Ash really was dead even though her brain told her he wasn't.

Someone knocked on the door. Bone couldn't move. She half expected the door to crack open and a plump little fox terrier to skitter in.

Where was Corolla? And Kiawah and Kitty Hawk? Where was Uncle Ash's truck?

It was not *him.*

Mrs. Price stuck her head in instead. "Bone, dear, come down to breakfast. You don't need to go to school, but you got to eat."

Bone groaned a response. Mrs. Price closed the door quietly. It took too much energy to argue or even say anything. Bone lay there listening to Mrs. P's footsteps echo across the hall and down the back steps. The radio played in the parlor, but it was soon drowned out by the clatter of dishes in the sink. Nothing else stirred in the house.

Had Uncle Junior gone to work? Had Miss Johnson? How could they go on like nothing had happened?

It wasn't him. It wasn't him.

Bone pulled herself out of bed. Her clothes lay on the floor, Mama's butter-yellow sweater and Uncle Ash's blue flannel shirt swaddled up together. Bone pulled on her dungarees—and his shirt. It was like a choir robe on her, swallowing her whole. She rolled the sleeves and tied the shirttails around her waist, comforted by the smells. She could see Ash running his hand down a horse's leg, feeling its pain. He laughed with Tiny over a smoke while Queenie's gelding cantered around the pasture. *Was that the last time he wore the shirt?* Ash was sticking his arm, sleeve rolled up, into a cow—and he pulled out a baby calf by its hooves. *"Just needed a bit of encouragement, didn't you?"* He laughed as the mama cow cleaned off the newborn and it struggled awkwardly to its feet. Uncle Ash wiped his hands on his shirt.

Ugh! That's why he didn't take the shirt to the beach! Bone stripped off the shirt, holding it out from her and dropping it back to the floor.

She pulled on her same old T-shirt and slipped into Mama's sweater. She saw Mama crying as a young Ash, a gangly teen, got on a bus headed north to Canada and the war. "I'll be home soon, Willow," he called out the window.

He did come home, of course, four years later—but a different man.

Bone buttoned the yellow sweater up to her throat before wiggling her feet into her boots. She tucked the poetry book into her back pocket.

Downstairs, a car door slammed and knocking pounded at the front door.

By the time Bone reached the kitchen, Mrs. Price was talking to someone in the parlor. Mamaw was furiously washing dishes. Uncle Junior sat at the linoleum-topped table, staring at the paper, his plate of eggs untouched.

"It's Mr. Matthews and the sheriff," Mrs. Price whispered as she came into the kitchen. "They want to talk to you," she said to Uncle Junior.

"Again?" He scraped his chair back and pulled himself to his feet, grabbing one last gulp of black coffee before facing them.

Mamaw wiped her hands. "Sit down, Bone, honey. I made you some oatmeal."

Mrs. Price pushed a bowl in front of Bone. She'd swirled a dollop of huckleberry jam into the creamy mixture.

Both women inched closer to the parlor, leaning in to listen. They didn't really need to. The mine supervisor's voice would cut through solid rock.

"Junior, I'm sorry for your loss," Mr. Matthews began. "And I realize this is a difficult time for your family—"

"As you know, we arrested Tiny Sherman for murdering your brother," the sheriff interrupted.

Bone pushed her oatmeal away, the bowl scraping against the linoleum tabletop.

Mrs. Price shushed her as Mamaw steamed into the parlor. Bone zigzagged past Mrs. Price to follow.

"You haven't yet proved that was Ash," Mamaw insisted.

Both the sheriff and Mr. Matthews gave Mamaw a pitying look—and turned to Uncle Junior.

"Have you figured out where he was killed?" he asked the sheriff.

"Um." Mr. Matthews blinked slowly. "What makes you think—"

"My brother never'd have gone down in the mine on his own, Mr. Matthews," Junior said. He turned to the sheriff. "Al, you remember what happened when Ash came back in '19."

"I know. That's what got me thinking foul play, too," the sheriff said. "The county medical examiner said the man died from getting hit from behind with something hard and flat, like a beam or a coal shovel."

The sheriff was being careful not to answer Uncle Junior's question, Bone couldn't help noticing. And Mr. Matthews kept fidgeting with the coins in his pocket.

Mr. Matthews coughed. "We don't need to go into those details in front of the women and children." He looked at Bone, and then away. "Trust me," he told Junior. "We're doing everything to make sure someone pays for your brother's death."

This time the sheriff coughed, and Mr. Matthews shut up.

"I had another look around shaft twenty-seven yesterday." The sheriff pulled something out of his coat pocket. It was a Memphis Red Sox cap. Tiny Sherman was the only person who wore one of those anywhere near Big Vein.

There was a long, uncomfortable silence in the parlor.

Bone couldn't figure it. These men—including Uncle Junior—thought Tiny Sherman killed his friend, her Uncle Ash, somewhere and then dragged him down the mine on the mantrip to where he and a bunch of other men were working—and then left his prize ball cap there. It was like a bad Charlie Chan or Bulldog Drummond movie.

"He could've left that there anytime," Junior finally said. "It's his job."

"Not anymore," Mr. Matthews said, shaking his head. "Never should've put my faith in that boy. I just promoted him to outside man and he goes and does something like this."

Mamaw glared a hole in the man.

"Why would Tiny do this?" Bone asked.

Mr. Matthews turned to her. "You never know with his kind, young lady."

"That's not what—," Bone stuttered in anger. Uncle Junior

63

put a hand on her shoulder. That was not what she meant at all. She'd meant Tiny had no reason to hurt Uncle Ash. It didn't make sense. They were friends.

Uncle Junior stood and stretched, poked at the fire for a moment. "One thing has been bothering me about this, Al." He turned to the sheriff, poker still in his hand. The tip of the iron was covered in ash.

"Just one?"

"We need to get the mine open and running today, Mr. Reed." Mr. Matthews tapped his watch. "You got more than enough evidence . . ."

The sheriff held up his hand. "Go on, Junior."

"The rock dust." Junior stirred the fireplace ashes once again before setting the poker back.

"The what?" Mr. Matthews asked.

Everyone looked at him. Even Bone knew what that was: the crushed limestone that the miners used to cut down the coal in the air so it wouldn't explode. Some folks called it lime, some rock dust.

"The body was covered with it when we found it." Junior studied first the sheriff, then Mr. Matthews as he said it. "Like someone had dusted the body down with a whole bag of lime."

The mine supervisor's face was a blank slate—until the last word.

"Oh, the lime!" Mr. Matthews said.

The sheriff nodded. "That is peculiar."

"Obviously, Tiny was just covering his tracks. The lime would eat away—I mean—destroy the evidence," Mr. Matthews said, pleased he'd thought of that. "They do that all the time in detective novels and films. He probably thought no one would find the body for a while."

"Uh-huh," Junior said, exchanging a glance with the sheriff, who just shook his head.

Mr. Matthews was right, though, at least about this. In one of Uncle Henry's detective novels she'd read, the killer covered the body in lime. The lime decomposed the body faster. What were Uncle Junior and the sheriff not saying?

"Now that we've got that mystery solved," Mr. Matthews charged on, "we got to open the mine again. The army needs coal!" He waggled his finger in Uncle Junior's face. "And if the army doesn't get it, we don't get paid."

"Hold your horses, Robinson Matthews," Mamaw told the mine superintendent. She turned, though, to the sheriff. "You didn't answer Bone's question. Why would Tiny kill—"

"What was his motive?" Bone clarified. *Motive* was the word they always used in detective novels.

The sheriff glanced at Mr. Matthews, who nodded. "Seems someone has been stealing coal. The night shift has come up short at the end of the week."

"Not all of the coal quite makes it onto the last train," Mr. Matthews said with a wry smile.

"What! You never told me," Uncle Junior rounded on Mr.

Matthews. "Or Tom Albert." Uncle Junior was the day shift supervisor, and Mr. Albert was the night shift super.

"You never know who's involved." Mr. Matthews's voice cracked a tiny bit, but he crossed his arms and stared at Uncle Junior.

"So you think Tiny and Ash were skimming off the last load?" Junior was gobsmacked.

"That's ludicrous! Neither Tiny nor Ash would do such a thing!" Mamaw backed Mr. Matthews into the settee. Uncle Junior wasn't far behind.

The sheriff didn't interfere. Bone watched him watching them.

"The thefts didn't start until Tiny was promoted. He's the one who runs the tipple and fills the orders," Mr. Matthews shot back. "And everyone knows Ash disappears this time of year. Probably off selling coal over the state line."

That was too much for Bone. "He goes to the beach!" she blurted out. To read poetry, she didn't say. From a book sent to him by a stranger. Bone pulled the book from her back pocket and clutched it to her. She saw a flash of a man pulling the book fresh from a shelf filled with other shiny leather covers. Through the store window, even shinier buildings loomed tall.

Mr. Matthews laughed and turned to her uncle. "I know you're not involved, Junior Reed. You and your daddy have served Superior Anthracite faithfully for many decades—and I'd hate for this to reflect badly on you in any way." Mr. Matthews was as slick as cat piss on linoleum.

He took a step toward Uncle Junior, ignoring Mamaw.

Junior trembled in anger, fixing to explode. Mamaw put a hand on his chest and said one word. "Don't."

"The sheriff is willing to keep Ash's name out of this affair. It was all Tiny, and Ash was just in the wrong place at the wrong time."

The sheriff sighed and nodded.

"Or it might come out that he wasn't the only Reed involved." Mr. Matthews said it with such satisfaction that Bone wanted to kick him. "And maybe it wasn't only the Reeds." He smiled at her as he took another step forward.

This time Uncle Junior backed off.

She got it now. The mine superintendent was threatening Uncle Junior's job—and maybe even Daddy's, too.

"I think y'all better leave. Now." Uncle Junior clipped out the words.

The two men headed toward the door.

Mamaw stood still, one hand on Junior's chest, holding back a dam that was about to burst. "Alfred, I'd like my boy's things."

Uncle Junior whispered something to her, and she added, "Including the dog tag."

Bone felt his eyes on her. He looked away.

"Yes, ma'am," the sheriff said quietly. "I'll have them back to you well before the funeral Sunday."

"Sunday?" Mamaw whipped around.

The bell jangled and the front door slammed shut.

"I haven't made arrangements yet—," she told Junior. "Mattie!" Mamaw stormed off.

The dog tag. He'd asked for the dog tag.

It was just her and Uncle Junior left in the parlor.

"I need to know it's him, for sure," he told Bone, still barely containing a rage she'd never seen. She knew it wasn't directed at her.

The thought of touching the dog tag cut through her like razor wire.

"And maybe you can tell . . ." he trailed off.

Who killed him.

"Bone, come finish your oatmeal," Mrs. Price called from the kitchen.

"I'm sorry, honey," Junior softened. "But I need to know."

She did, too. She still didn't think it was Uncle Ash, but what if it were? The thought of seeing anyone, let alone her favorite person in the whole wide world, dying horribly felt like it was going to suffocate her.

She had to get out. Into the wide-openest, free-est space she could find.

The bell jangled over the front door as Bone bolted toward Flat Woods.

8

BONE RACED DOWN THE GRAVEL ROAD and into the woods that ran from the river up to the mine. She'd seen death in other objects. A deer struck by an arrow. A young boy drowning. Will's father buried in the mine. Mama.

It's not him, she reminded herself.

Bone stumbled over a root, sending her and the poetry book sprawling into an ancient foxhole. She lay there, watching her breath hang in the crisp air, staring up past the bare treetops at the cold blue sky. Back during another war, the men of Big Vein had dug these holes to hide from Confederate press-gangs. Before dawn, the men would cover themselves with leaves and branches and wait out the day. At night, they'd return home to plow their fields and visit with their families. Come daylight, they were back out here, lying in the ground like they were in their graves already. The cold of the earth began to seep into her bones. She grabbed Uncle Ash's book, and she felt his rising panic seeping through the leather cover. Big guns shook the ground, dirt cascaded on top of him, and an explosion nearby sealed off the light. Bone sprang to her feet. Shaking off the vision, she slid the book into her back pocket.

Bone crawled out and brushed the dried leaves from her britches and sweater. She picked her way across the minefield of holes and downed branches toward the river—and Picnic Rock. There she climbed up on the flat boulder and sat cross-legged, watching the river ripple by below. The sound washed away some of the images in her head.

She carefully pulled out Uncle Ash's book and read his favorite poem aloud. She saw him reading on the beach, feeling peaceful yet sad. *When did he get this?* A younger Ash, maybe nineteen or twenty, held a brown paper parcel addressed to him in neat handwritten letters. He snipped the string with his pocketknife and unwrapped the book. Its leather cover shone. He checked the paper again. No return address. The postmark said Chicago. Uncle Ash smiled.

He knew who sent the book! But Bone couldn't pick it out of his thoughts.

Uncle Ash had asked her to find out who sent this. Another man cracked open the spine of the little volume, feeling the same peaceful sadness. He gently closed the book and laid it on a store counter. Bone couldn't see what this man looked like.

Twigs snapped behind her.

Will came walking down through the woods from the direction of the mine.

Below them, dogs barked as they chased something through the woods. Mr. Childress must be running his dogs.

"What are you doing out here?" Bone asked. Not that she minded Will's company.

He hopped up on the rock beside her. "Tipple."

Ever since he'd started talking again, which was only since Halloween, Will had been frugal with his words. Bone still knew what he meant. He'd been snooping around where that mess of coal was left Saturday night. "Find anything?"

He shook his head. "The boys done too good a job cleaning up."

Bone had an awful thought. "The sheriff said that person was killed somewhere else and dragged down into the mine. Do you think . . ." She couldn't finish it.

Will nodded this time. "The tipple."

A pile of coal was left there after the last train on Saturday night. The boys said it had been happening for a month or so now. It had to be connected to the body. Maybe that person had seen who was stealing coal.

"We should stake out the tipple after the 8:15," Bone said.

"Saturday?" Will considered—and then nodded. "Jake and Clay, too."

Bone agreed. They'd know exactly where under the tipple to watch.

She felt better now that they were doing something, anything.

Will tapped the book cover.

"It's Uncle Ash's." She opened it and read his favorite poem aloud again.

The words and the burble of the river below washed away Bone's doubts, for now.

9

THE NEXT MORNING, MAMAW WAS WAITING for Bone in the kitchen with a plate of scrambled eggs and two cups of mint tea sweetened with honey.

"I'm going stir-crazy down here," Mamaw announced, setting down her cup. "And I got work to do. And you need something to do, too."

Bone shook her head. "I can't go to school yet." She couldn't bear the thought of carrying on like nothing had ever happened. The mine was up and running again. Uncle Junior was back at work. Mattie and Ruby were packing boxes. It just didn't seem right, even if it wasn't Uncle Ash. A man had died. Mr. Sherman was in jail. And, besides, all those folks going about their business really did think Uncle Ash was dead. It wasn't right. It wasn't him. But it still wasn't right.

"No, you're coming with me," Mamaw said, dangling a set of car keys in front of Bone. "After you finish them eggs."

Outside, Aunt Mattie's black Ford was parked by the curb.

"Do you even know how to drive, Mamaw?" Bone asked. Uncle Ash always drove her everywhere. Or she walked.

Mamaw practically hooted. "Who do you think taught Ash and Mattie? Or your mama or Junior? Your Papaw didn't have time, between working in the mine and hauling shine back in the day." She opened the door. "And sometimes I helped with that, too." She winked.

"What?" Bone had heard Mamaw and Ash talk about Papaw's still, but she hadn't thought he made it for anything more than medicinal purposes. "Shine? You mean he actually sold it? And you drove it?"

She didn't answer. Mamaw slid into the driver's seat and pushed the starter button. The '39 Ford roared to life. Bone hopped in the car and shut the door, afraid Mamaw would leave her behind. The inside of the plain sedan gleamed, the mahogany dash looking brand new.

Mamaw chuckled. "Your aunt doesn't realize she's driving a hot rod. Perfect for running shine." She gunned the engine before throwing the car in gear. "Drives like she's afraid of what's under the hood." Mamaw tore down the road toward the river. "It's a V-8."

Bone gripped the door handle. Mamaw slowed down to a reasonable pace as they neared the river. She parked at the ferry landing. Mr. Goodwin started the ferry up moving from the other side of the river.

"Papaw's old Model T is still in the barn under a bunch of tarps. I might have to get Mattie to see if she could get it running again before she starts her new job." Mamaw fell quiet.

Was Mamaw giving up? She'd need a car or truck to get by if Uncle Ash was truly gone. Aunt Mattie was moving away, and Uncle Junior didn't have a car. Neither did Daddy. Where was Uncle Ash's truck? And the dogs?

As the ferry docked on their side, Mr. Goodwin waved to them. "I didn't think that was the preacher's wife tearing down the road."

Bone hopped out and caught the bowline as he threw it. Mamaw drove the Ford onto the rickety ferry like an old hand. The wooden deck bobbed in the current with the added weight. Mr. Goodwin reached a hand to pull Bone on board. They were across the river and up the road without much conversation.

The Ford climbed Reed Mountain, the Virginia pines almost a blur along the twisty road. Bone relaxed her grip on the door handle and hung her head out the window. The cold sand blasted her skin and the world smelled evergreen.

The Ford slowed as it passed over the little bridge. They were now on Reed land. The fields on one side of the drive had been mowed and the hay put up. On the other side, the gardens had been neatly turfed, with only a patch or two of winter vegetables—dark leafy kale, mostly—left around Mamaw's little cabin. Bone knew the root cellars were probably full, too. The chickens scratched and pecked under the main house, a giant treehouse really, built between four massive oaks.

Mamaw parked by her cabin; she called it her office. Bone thought of it as more of a laboratory. Three calico cats rushed to greet Mamaw. Sassafras and her kittens, Savory and Sage. "I know, my darlings," she clucked as she let them in the cabin. At the door, people had left flowers and food as well as notes and even a bottle of whiskey. Mamaw scooped up the notes—and the whiskey. Bone brought in the rest.

Inside, the shelves lining the walls were fully stocked. Little sacks of dried leaves and herbs. Jars of tinctures and syrups. Tins of salves.

"We've got some orders—and the offer of a truck," Mamaw said matter-of-factly.

Bone put the food in the icebox and the flowers in the sink.

"Lucy Riddle has a bad cough. Mrs. Teague has woman problems. And Malcolm Hicks wrenched his shoulder," Mamaw read from the notes, sorting them into piles. "Bone, get me a small bottle of elderberry syrup and weigh out a quarter pound of red clover. I'll get the fixings for a salve ready."

She seemed happy, or at least content, to be back at work. The smells of the cabin were comforting and familiar. Sprigs of lavender and rosemary hung from the rafters—as did cloves of garlic and strings of fiery peppers. Hints of mint and earth from the gardens haunted the air.

Bone crossed the room to the syrup section. In winter, Mamaw devoted several shelves to elderberry syrups and tinctures. Bone had helped her press and bottle at least half of them. She unscrewed the cap on a small bottle. It smelled like blueberry pie, albeit a garlicky one. The syrup would cut any cough.

Next, Bone located the red clover. She weighed out the dry leaves on the scale next to the workbench. As she poured it in a paper sack, she watched Mamaw. Humming, she laid out beeswax, a bottle of greenish oil, and some little glass jars on the workbench. Mamaw could happily lose herself in this work, whether it was making a tincture or growing herbs or studying a plant with her Gift.

Bone couldn't see herself lost and happy in her own Gift, not like Mamaw and Uncle Ash were in theirs. Neither of them might have to watch someone they love die as part of their Gift. Even as she thought this, Bone half expected Uncle Ash to come bursting through the door with Corolla.

"Let me show you how to make a salve," Mamaw said as she eyed one of the glass jars. "Shame I can't get the tins no more. Folks turned them all in to the scrap drive."

On the little woodstove, she already had the double boiler going. "Melt some of that beeswax," Mamaw told Bone.

Bone plopped two hunks of the wax into the top pan, stirring it occasionally as it melted.

"Now slowly pour a cup of this infused oil into the beeswax." Mamaw handed her a measuring cup half full of the green liquid.

She swirled it into the wax, stirring it with the wooden spoon until it was smooth. The hot concoction smelled like cut grass. "What's in this?"

"Boneset. It's good for pain. Some say it helps bones set." Mamaw held the jar in her hand. "It helps things knit together. Kind of like you, honey." She peered over Bone's shoulder.

Bone liked the idea of being nicknamed after something other than the worthless rock coal miners threw out. And doing something useful that helped people. Who was going to take over once Mamaw was gone?

"Okay, now you open up the jars while I pour."

Bone obliged, and Mamaw poured in the greenish wax. It quickly started to cloud up and harden.

"Mamaw?" Bone inhaled the grassy aroma of the salve. She wasn't quite sure how to ask this.

"Hmm?" Mamaw was busy scraping the pan clean.

"Have you been teaching me things so I can take over from you?"

The pan clattered in the sink, and Mamaw turned to study Bone. "No, not as such." She wiped her hands on a dish towel. "If you really wanted to know, of course, I'd teach you everything." She motioned for Bone to sit at the big table. She used the hot water still burbling on the stove to make cups of tea.

Then she scrounged sugar cookies from a tin someone had left on the doorstep.

"Bone, honey, even before my Gift came on, I loved plants. Growing them. Picking wild ones. Knowing all about them and how to use them. I always thought the idea that you could put a teensy little seed in the ground and grow beauty and medicine and food was all magical." Mamaw practically glowed as she talked. "Then my Gift was just . . . gravy on top of a perfect biscuit."

Bone laughed at the comparison. White sausage gravy on a fluffy biscuit tasted darn good—but not magical.

"Or snow on Christmas Day." Mamaw bit into one of the cookies. "I want that for you, Bone."

"But . . ." She searched for the words. "But my Gift is hardly gravy or even a fluffy biscuit."

Mamaw chuckled. "That's true. You've got a hard Gift, Forever Girl. Hard as the dirt under our feet."

Bone nodded, grateful that Mamaw understood. Her Gift wasn't as easy as looking into a plant to see what it could do or into an animal to know what's wrong with it. She saw people at their worst moments. She saw them at their best, too. But she also saw them die.

"What did you love most in the world before your Gift came on?"

"Stories." Bone didn't hesitate. "Still do."

"What do the objects tell you?"

"Stories," Bone admitted. "But what do I do with them?"

Mamaw raised an eyebrow at Bone while she sipped her tea.

"I know." She'd known the answer as soon as the question had left her mouth. The objects tell her how to help people, too. She'd figured out what happened to Mama. She'd helped Will get his voice back. Now she needed to help Uncle Ash. Or whoever that was.

And Mr. Sherman.

But she'd also known *what to do* wasn't the real problem either. "Mamaw, I can't bear some of the stories," she finally said. *Especially if they're about Uncle Ash dying.*

"Ah, Bone, honey," Mamaw said. "You're kindly like that hot rod Mattie drives. Don't be afraid of the power under your own hood."

It wasn't the power she was afraid of, exactly. It was feeling all those bad things—like she did when she saw Mama die. She lost her all over again, and it about drowned her. She wasn't ready to feel that way again, especially about Uncle Ash.

It wasn't him. *It wasn't him.*

"You've had more than your fair share of loss." Mamaw took her hand. "But I expect that's another reason how come you got this Gift. You're strong, and what you've been through will help you help other folks."

"Help tell their stories?" Bone sighed. That was easier said than done. But it was *her* Gift. And if Uncle Ash was truly gone, she'd want his story told. She'd want to tell it herself.

Mamaw kissed Bone's forehead as she rose to pour herself another cup of tea.

"Who will take over all this?" Bone swept her hand around the cabin. Not only did the shelves brim with the fruits of Mamaw's labor, but folks needed her. They drove from all over to get a salve to ease their arthritis, a syrup to fight a cold, or a tea to help with their monthlies.

"I'd hoped one of my granddaughters would've had the same Gift." Mamaw pushed a white cookie toward Bone. "But Poppy, Queenie's granddaughter, wants to learn."

That made Bone happy. All this magic her grandmother grew, distilled, infused, and loved shouldn't disappear from the world. And Poppy had the right name for the job.

The cookies tasted like butter and the tea like peppermint. That made her think of Uncle Ash again. "I keep expecting him to come through that back door with Corolla."

Mamaw nodded. "I was thinking the same thing."

Bone needed to read that dog tag. She needed to tell his story.

10

BY THE TIME MAMAW DROPPED Bone at the boarding-house, the sheriff had come and gone.

And Uncle Junior was waiting for her—alone—in the parlor. The fire crackled, and the radio was playing the war news.

He opened his hand. A single round pewter dog tag with bits of leather cord lay in his palm. The tag said SGT ASH REED on it sure enough.

Bone had seen one like it around Uncle Ash's neck many a time. He probably hadn't taken it off since the Great War.

"Uncle Ash told me never to touch them." She knew she needed to, though.

Junior clenched the tag in his fist. "I know it's asking a lot, Bone. I've thought long and hard about this. I'd never ask it if I didn't think it was him." He opened his hand again, the outline of the tag dug into his palm like a trench. "I need to know who killed Ash."

She'd thought about it, too. She'd thought about how horrible it would be to see her favorite person in the world die. She shook herself. It wasn't him. But she needed to know for sure—for herself, for Uncle Junior, and for Mr. Sherman.

Bone held her hand over the tag. A powerful wave of feelings hit her. Surprise. Blackness. Anger. Sadness. It had a familiar yet foreign feel at the same time. She snatched her hand back.

"Bone?" Uncle Junior asked quietly. "I'm sorry. You don't have to do this." He took the dog tag back.

Bone held her hand out, and he gently placed the disk in hers.

Images flooded her. She took a deep breath and asked a question, just like Uncle Ash had taught her. *What happened to you?* In the darkness, something rumbled. Rocks, coal fell like a black waterfall. Then came nothingness. Bone pushed back a little farther back. *Where were you before this?* The heat was sweltering in a small, cramped space. Men laughed. Loud music thundered over the roar of an engine. Everything felt like it was going to smother him . . . her. Standing, the wearer popped his head up into the fresh, yet still sweltering air. Bone felt his exhilaration as they raced and bounced across enormous sand dunes. He licked the salt from his lips. The sand blasted his skin, but he didn't care. He was free as a dog running along a beach. Sweat rolled down Bone's face.

Then everything jerked to a stop—and he wasn't free anymore. Men in different uniforms pointed guns at him—and he didn't seem entirely unhappy about it.

Who are you? She still couldn't really see his face.

A fair-haired woman twirled by in a wedding dress. Towheaded children kicked a ball across a green field, strange black dogs bounding with them after it. A blur of stone buildings. Singing. Snowcapped mountains in the background. Men drinking big glasses of beer. And uniforms Bone didn't recognize.

"Is it Ash?" Uncle Junior whispered.

Bone was about to shake her head. Then the scene shifted as if in answer to his question. Snow fell on muddy trenches. Running, dogs on his heels. The mud splatting as bullets whizzed into the sides of the trench. Mortars exploding. Deafening roar. Diving into a hole. Loud thud overhead. Rumbling. Darkness. Panic. Guns echoing above.

Bone set the dog tag down. They were the guns in Uncle Ash's head, what he'd heard when he was trapped in the tunnel.

"I see the Battle of Cambrai . . ." She saw so much else, though. Someone else?

Uncle Junior sunk to the floor.

"There's other stuff that doesn't make sense," Bone said. But Uncle Ash was wearing this tag when he'd gotten buried alive in that tunnel in 1917. The other memories came after that, didn't they? Where did they come from? Had Uncle Ash been in the desert? Bone picked up the tag again, holding it just by the leather cord. She pictured Uncle Ash worrying his dog tags whenever he talked about the war, which wasn't often.

Dog tags. Plural.

"Where's his other tag?" Bone asked. Uncle Ash wore two tags, one like this and the other a bit bigger. She could see him tucking them into his red flannel shirt—and lighting a shaky Lucky Strike.

Uncle Junior looked up, a glint of hope in his eyes.

Bone told him about the other things she'd seen. The desert. The woman. The kids. The dogs.

"You've got the damnedest Gift, Bone," he said, pulling himself to his feet. "That last part don't sound like Ash."

Bone threw up her hands in confusion. She couldn't see the wearer clearly. That puzzled her. The last memories didn't feel like Uncle Ash's, though.

"Did you see who killed him?" Uncle Junior whispered.

She asked the tag. It showed her a train pulling away. The man stepped out of the darkness, and something hit him from behind. Then the coal fell.

But one thing was sure. The wearer died under the tipple at Big Vein.

That's the only place rocks or coal rained down like water.

11

BONE COULDN'T SLEEP for thinking about what she'd seen
in that dog tag. It was telling her a jumbled-up jigsaw puzzle of
a story—with big chunks missing. She leafed through the pieces
in her mind, turning them every which way trying to force them
together. Finally, she grasped at an edge piece: what happened
at the tipple. She could start there. She needed to know more
about it, and Jake and Clay had cleaned up a mess of coal under
the tipple two days later.

Bone lay in bed until she heard Uncle Junior quietly go down
the stairs. Mrs. Price was stirring in the kitchen making his breakfast. Bone quickly got dressed and crept down the back stairs.

Mrs. Price flipped eggs over in the cast-iron skillet, bacon
sizzling alongside them. Bone's stomach grumbled.

"Bone, what are you doing up at the crack of dawn?" Uncle Junior asked over the morning paper. He was wearing his bank clothes, and his dinner bucket sat on the counter, waiting for him.

"Couldn't sleep," Bone answered. She touched the bucket lightly, bracing herself, but all she saw was Uncle Junior sitting in the cut in the near dark, eating a fried bologna sandwich, the beam from his headlamp bouncing off the dark walls of the mine as he laughed at a story Daddy told him. When he was done eating, he wiped away the crumbs and laid one hand on the dank surface of a wall. Inside his head, he could see dark veins of coal spidering through the mountain. "We need to blast up thataway," he told Daddy. And they did.

Bone smiled seeing a glimpse of Uncle Junior's Gift in action.

Mrs. Price laid a plate of eggs and bacon in front of Uncle Junior and another in front of her own place at the table. "What can I get you, honey?"

"Bacon and maybe some toast," Bone said, slipping into her chair. She didn't think she could stomach the eggs, but the bacon did smell good.

Mrs. Price took the bacon and toast off her plate and set it on one for Bone.

Uncle Junior poked at his egg as he read the paper. Bone nibbled her toast while Mrs. Price dropped more bacon into the pan.

"Uncle Junior?" Bone asked.

"Hmm?" He looked up from the war news.

"How does the tipple work?" There was still something

88

niggling at Bone about the whole business under the tipple, besides of course somebody dying under it.

Uncle Junior laid the paper down. "It loads the coal on the trains."

"I know, but how?" Bone bit into a crisp piece of bacon.

Mrs. Price exchanged a look with Uncle Junior as she refilled his coffee.

Uncle Junior stared at Bone for a moment before the light bulb came on. "Why don't you walk me to work?" He gulped down his coffee as he rose. Mrs. Price handed him his lunch pail—and an extra piece of toast—as he pulled on his jacket. "We can talk shop on the way."

Bone gobbled down the rest of her bacon before grabbing her coat from the peg in the back hallway.

~

Outside, the sky was still coal black, and the air was sharp. Right airish, some folks would call it. The gravel crunched under their feet as they walked up the road to the mine.

"You thinking about what you saw?" Uncle Junior asked.

"Yes. Pieces of the story don't fit together. It's like Uncle Ash wore the tag, but so did a completely different person." Bone turned up the collar of her coat. "But whoever it was, he died under the tipple."

Soon they were standing in front of the mine—and the sun was just beginning to peek over the mountain to the east. Uncle

Junior clicked on his mining lamp and shone it at the tipple. The structure stretched across the train tracks and one lane of gravel road like a covered bridge over a small stream.

"Some part of the tipple runs most of the time during a shift. We fill up the mine cars down below, and a conveyor belt carries them up from the mine. We used to have to send them up there and tip them over ourselves. That's why it's called a tipple." Uncle Junior pointed to the side of the covered bridge-like structure that was closest to the mine. "Nowadays the outside man throws a lever, and the mine car opens up and drops its load into the crusher. It breaks the coal down into different-sized pieces, and they get sorted and washed. Then they get dumped into holding bins, waiting on the trains and trucks." He shone his light on the part of the bridge over the tracks. "When a train or truck comes, the outside man flips another lever to load the hoppers and drop the coal."

Right now, the conveyors, crushers, and bins were quiet.

"Anybody ever stolen coal off the tipple?" Bone studied the tipple. She'd seen it a thousand times but never really looked at it. Somehow getting to the coal this way didn't seem likely—or else it was a lot of work.

"Not that I recall." Uncle Junior studied the tipple, too. "But during the Depression folks stole it right off the trains. Usually when they were in the railyard or on a side spur like this one. Sometimes the railroad leaves coal cars on the spur until there's enough to make the trip worthwhile."

The coal cars were never covered. Someone could easily scoop up some coal at night from a parked train—or one that was being loaded.

"You going to school?" Junior asked. He shone his light on Bone.

She shrugged. She still wanted to talk to Jake and Clay, but she didn't want to sit through class all day.

Uncle Junior clicked off his mining lamp. "I'll do a little snooping myself," he added thoughtfully. "Something's bothering me about this, too." He pecked her on the forehead and headed toward the change house.

~⁀͜~

Bone lingered, staring at the tipple as the early fingers of sunlight began to illuminate it.

If someone was stealing coal, why not take it off a parked coal car? Stealing off the tipple, even late on a Saturday night, seemed like more trouble than it was worth. And somebody was bound to have seen something. Perhaps somebody did.

Bone walked back to the school and parked herself on one of the picnic tables.

Ruby and the Little Jewels were coming up the road, bundled against the chill. Ruby stopped but waved Opal and Pearl to go on in.

"How can you go to school like nothing happened?" Bone asked.

91

Ruby frowned. "Mother is forcing me," she said finally. "She wants to make sure Robbie Matthews asks me to the dance."

Bone sprang off the picnic table. "How can she be thinking about that now?" Aunt Mattie obviously didn't care a wit about Uncle Ash, her own brother. How could she ever have declared a truce with Mattie?

"Really, I think she just wants me out of the house." Ruby shivered. "Coming in?"

Bone shook her head. "Tell Jake and Clay to meet me Saturday night after supper. Me and Will are going to stake out the tipple." It felt good to at least be doing something.

Ruby started to answer, but Robbie Matthews sidled up beside her. "I got something to ask you," he told her, ignoring Bone. He guided Ruby toward the classroom door.

"I'll tell them," Ruby called over her shoulder.

Bone stomped back toward the boardinghouse. She had half a mind to stop by the parsonage and give Aunt Mattie another piece of her mind.

She didn't.

12

MRS. PRICE KEPT BONE BUSY most of Friday and Saturday, baking, cleaning, and washing clothes for the impending funeral. It was just as well. All she could think about, all she wanted to think about, was solving this mystery. Who was this man? What happened to him?

It was not Uncle Ash—even though folks were going to bury that body like it was him.

Come Saturday evening, Will knocked on the back door of the boardinghouse as usual. She slipped out without anyone noticing. They were all lost in their own thoughts.

Uncle Ash would've noticed—and probably followed them.

Jake and Clay—and, to Bone's surprise, Ruby—were waiting up the road. Ruby held out a thermos. "Hot chocolate," she whispered. It was chilly, and the breeze blowing down the mountain was icy. Ruby shivered in her skirt and bare legs, but she did bring an old blanket.

"Bet you wish you owned a pair of dungarees about now," Bone whispered back.

Will pointed to the woods and pressed a finger to his lips.

"Hot dog." Jake elbowed Clay. "We're gonna be regular Sherlock Holmeses."

"Hush," Bone told the Sherlocks and herded them toward the trees. Once they were a few feet into the woods, Bone flicked on the flashlight. Will led the way to the spot he'd staked out on the edge of the woods across from the tipple. Bone clicked off the light, and Ruby spread out the blanket. The boys scoffed at it—until they had sat on the cold ground for about five minutes. Soon everyone was crowded on the blanket. Will shaded the light as he checked his watch: 8:07. The only sounds were the river below—and the distant chug of the train still miles away.

"Will," Bone said. "Something's been bothering me about what Mr. Matthews said."

Will cocked his head to one side.

"You found the body and it had rock dust all over it. Mr. M said it would eat away the body like in the movies."

Jake laughed, and Clay socked him on the arm.

"Shush," Ruby said.

"Why's that funny?" Bone whispered.

Will whispered back, "Rock dust ain't the same as quicklime."

"Rock dust is ground-up limestone," Clay explained.

"Miners get that on them all the time," Jake said. "Doesn't eat their faces off."

"Oh!" Bone said. "But quicklime would?"

Will nodded.

Somebody evidently thought covering the body in rock dust would destroy the evidence. That somebody, though, didn't know the difference between lime and quicklime.

"Don't think the mine even has quicklime anymore," Clay said. In the old days, he explained, quicklime was used to break up rock—before dynamite. Some folks used it mixed in fertilizer or to tan hides, too.

"How did Mr. Matthews not know the difference?" Ruby asked.

This time Will laughed. "Never seen him down the mines."

The boys agreed. "Never saw him up top neither," Jake added.

Big surprise that Robbie Matthews's father didn't know what he was talking about.

Will tapped his watch again: 8:13.

Moonlight shone on the tipple.

A screech shattered the silence.

Ruby about jumped out of her skin, spilling hot chocolate on Jake.

"It's just a barn owl," Bone whispered.

"I knew that." Ruby dabbed up the hot chocolate with the edge of the blanket.

"Well, I about peed my pants," Clay said.

Jake punched him in the shoulder. "Me, too. Granddaddy says they're an omen of death."

Will leaned in. "Knock, knock."

"Who's there?" Bone asked.

"Owl."

"Owl who?"

"Owl be glad when this train finally comes."

Clay groaned.

Jake punched Will on the shoulder. "That was terrible, man."

Ruby covered her mouth. And Bone actually smiled. This was the best she'd felt in days.

Will's bad owl joke put her in mind of the one he'd told his daddy when he was little. He'd told the knock-knock joke into the jelly jar, the one his father had with him when he died. Will didn't talk after that, not until Bone figured out how to free his voice from that jelly jar. As Uncle Ash would say, that was a whole 'nuther story.

Will tapped his watch. The train was making its way around the bend, its brakes beginning to quietly squeal as it slowed down. The tipple whirled to life, lights flicking on and the conveyor motor grinding. It shook as it sorted and dropped coal into its hoppers, getting ready for the train.

As it approached, a brakeman jumped out of the locomotive's

cab and waved the train under the tipple with his lantern. He signaled the outside man in the tipple, and then coal thundered down into one car. The train screeched forward. Another car filled. And then another. It took almost an hour to fill all the cars with coal.

Jake, Clay, and Ruby fell asleep. Bone ran everything she'd seen in that dog tag over and over in her head. The rumble of the coal falling through the tipple chute matched what she'd heard.

Finally, the brakeman hopped onto the back of the caboose as it pulled under the tipple. No doubt he'd hop off again in a few hundred yards to switch the train back to the main line. The coal train chugged east toward the port in Norfolk—and the war. The tipple shut down.

Bone elbowed the others awake.

No truck appeared.

Nothing happened for several very long minutes.

The barn owl screeched again.

Then a large black dog the size of a yearling walked out of the shadows. The dog stood directly under the tipple. Its big saucer eyes glinted in the moonlight—and fixed themselves on Bone.

One of the boys gulped hard, and someone whimpered.

Bone stood up. She'd never seen a dog like that, black, muscular, with pointy ears, though there was something familiar about it. Was it like the dogs she'd seen in the tag?

The others rose behind her. She took a step toward the dog—and it vanished.

Ruby gasped.

"I really am going to pee myself now," Clay whispered.

"It was a ghost dog," Bone marveled. A real-life spirit dog just like in Uncle Ash's stories. And the Swift's Mine tale. She flicked on the flashlight and motioned for the others to follow.

"More like a devil dog with them ears," Clay said.

"Do you think there's some treasure buried here?" Jake asked.

This time Ruby socked him in the arm.

"Ow."

Bone walked to the very spot the dog had stood.

"This is where we cleaned up that pile of coal last Monday morning," Clay said, kicking at the spot. There wasn't any loose coal this time.

Will let out a low appreciative whistle.

Uncle Ash always said spirit dogs could come as a warning, a harbinger of death, or a bringer of justice. Or it could be like that dog in the Swift's Mine story, guarding something precious. Bone had the distinct feeling, though, this dog was trying to tell her something. "Whoever Will found in shaft twenty-seven had gotten himself killed right here where we're standing," Bone declared.

No one argued with her.

A real-life devil dog was guarding the spot. And it wasn't one of Ash's dogs, neither.

Bone and her friends walked back home down the mine road in the near silence, the only sounds being the river below and the train disappearing in the distance.

"Y'all looking for that truck?" a voice called out of the darkness.

"Dang it, I really am going to pee myself before the night is through," Clay exclaimed.

A figure stepped out into the moonlight, followed closely by a couple of hound dogs. It was Mr. Childress. His two dogs cowered behind him. "Fool dogs won't go near that tipple no more."

"Truck?" Bone asked.

"Didn't come tonight." Mr. Childress fell in beside them. He explained how Saturday for a month or more, a truck had come rattling along the road past his place after the last train. Mr. Childress lived a few houses down and was known to sit out on his porch every night, playing his fiddle. "Thought I'd walk the dogs a bit and see for myself what was going on."

Perhaps the truck didn't come tonight because the driver or his accomplice was lying in a coffin at the funeral home.

"What about last Saturday?" Bone asked. "Did you see it then?"

"Yes, about 9:30 or near to ten o'clock, a truck came tearing down the road—with no lights on."

"What kind of truck did you see, Uncle Nate?" Will asked. Mr. Childress was Will's great-uncle on his mama's side.

Mr. Childress shook his head. "I cannot get over you talking,

Will Kincaid. You sound just like your daddy." He took a moment to light his pipe. "Oh, it were a big dumper truck like the ones the mine runs. Reckon that's why I didn't think much of it at first."

"Did you see who was driving?" Bone asked.

"Nah, it weren't your Uncle Ash or Tiny Sherman, though, that's for damn sure."

"But you didn't see the man," Ruby said.

Bone gave Ruby the stink eye, but she had to admit it was a good question.

"No," Mr. Childress finally allowed.

Will started to say something.

"It's not him," Bone said. It was not Uncle Ash. Not in the truck. Not in the coffin. Even if that dog tag belonged to him.

Ruby, the boys, and Mr. Childress said their good nights, leaving Bone and Will to walk back to the boardinghouse in silence. He was itching to say something, she could tell, but she didn't want to hear it.

"You think it's him, don't you?" Bone finally asked, as she stood on the back steps.

Will struggled to find the words. "The ghost dog," Will managed. Then he got out his pencil and wrote something in his little notebook.

He handed her the slip.

Who else would leave it to warn us? To warn you?

Will had her there. She didn't think it worked that way. But if it did, Uncle Ash would certainly send her a ghost dog.

100

13

UNCLE JUNIOR WAS WAITING for her on the front porch steps. And he was smoking, something he'd given up years ago. "Having one for Ash," he said with a cough. "Don't know how he still does it." Junior stubbed out the cigarette on the step. "But it's got something to do with this." He had the dog tag in his other hand. His beat-up old guitar leaned against the railing. "Maybe if I'd served . . ."

Uncle Junior had gotten turned away at the draft office. Flat feet.

Bone held out her hand. "I need to see it again," she demanded.

"You sure?" He handed it to her without waiting for an answer.

Bone clenched the tag in her hand, still mad at Will. It wasn't him. There had to be another explanation. This time she got nothing. "Dang it!" The one time she actually wanted to see something. She plopped herself down on the step next to Uncle Junior.

"What's got you madder than a hornet?" Junior asked. "Will say something?"

Bone didn't answer.

"Sometimes when I'm angry, my Gift don't work either," Junior said. "Take a deep breath—and tell me what he said."

Bone sucked in her breath and let it out. "He thinks it's Uncle Ash."

"You still don't?" Junior picked up his guitar and strummed a few soft chords. "Mama is still convinced it ain't. And I don't know what to think." He ran his thumb over the strings. "You know what? It does not matter. The law, the church, and your Aunt Mattie are fixing to bury Ash Reed on the weight of that one dog tag—no matter what we think."

Whatever she saw in the tag's story wasn't exactly proof the sheriff would believe.

"Now that you're home, I'm going to turn in . . . unless you want me to sit with you some."

Bone shook her head.

Uncle Junior rose and pecked her on the forehead. "Don't stay out here too late. We got to get to the church early in the morning . . ."

Uncle Ash's funeral was tomorrow.

The night was nearly silent. The wind rustled through bare trees across the road, and the river murmured over its rocks in the distance.

Was Will right? Is that why the ghost dog came?

Bone closed her eyes and pictured the ghost dog, with its gleaming eyes, black coat, and pointy ears. Except for the eyes, it looked like the dogs she'd seen in the tag. It tingled in her hand. She opened her palm. Coal fell from the tipple. A shadowy figure swung a shovel. Blackness and falling. Then the man was being dragged, blackness again. He woke pinned in the darkness, blood pouring down his face. He was thinking of his boys and his wife, the white-capped mountains near his home, and his own dogs, the black ones, longing for one to come dig him out like one did so long ago—or at least to bring his killer to justice.

The devil dog came when he called. Whoever he was.

It was not Uncle Ash.

Relief washed over Bone like a cool breeze. She squeezed the dog tag tight in her palm, silently thanking her Gift.

14

THE WORLD SWIRLED AROUND BONE as the pallbearers carried the coffin slowly up to the front of the church. Mamaw grabbed her elbow in a viselike grip. She stood straight as a poplar tree, only swaying ever so slightly in the breeze. Bone felt instantly grounded. She clutched the poetry book in front of her, the dog tag pressed between its pages like a flower. Even through her white gloves, she could feel the turmoil in the objects.

"It ain't him," Bone whispered to Mamaw.

Mamaw gave her elbow a tiny squeeze and let her go. "You saw something else?" she asked in a hushed voice.

Bone nodded. "It doesn't all make sense, though." She'd lain awake trying to fit the puzzle pieces together—and not all of them fit. Uncle Ash had worn that dog tag—at least up to some point in the Great War. Then the memories became different. She'd seen the woman, the black dogs, one baby, and then another. She'd seen him hunched over a table, pen in one hand, T-shaped ruler in the other, losing himself in sketching plans for a thirty-story building. Definitely not Uncle Ash. Bone still couldn't untangle all of the memories—or make sense of the very last ones, except to be sure the man wearing the tags had gotten clobbered under the tipple. Right on that spot the devil dog appeared. And then he was dragged down into the mine. Alive. And he was trapped, like he had been all those years ago, drowning in the darkness.

Bone shuddered. It was closing in on her, too, fixing to squeeze the life out of her.

The pallbearers gently set the box down in front of the pulpit. Uncle Junior, Uncle Henry's brother, cousin Ivy's husband, and several of Uncle Ash's friends and customers returned to their seats, heads bowed. They filed past, caps in hand, nodding to Mamaw and Bone. Uncle Junior straightened the coffin, and then slipped into the pew next to Bone. Ruby and Mattie, Bone finally noticed, were sitting on the opposite side of the aisle—with the Matthews family.

Bone nudged Mamaw and glared in Aunt Mattie's direction. Mamaw arched an eyebrow at her daughter but didn't say a word.

The service went by in a blur. The new preacher, Mr. Stewart, said some words about Uncle Ash's service in the Great War. The new man had come in early to perform the service. His family was still back in Norfolk packing up their belongings to move into the parsonage next month.

"I wrote to the army to get Mr. Reed's service record," the preacher said. He pulled out a letter and began reading from it. "'Sergeant Ash Reed volunteered in 1914, enlisting in the Canadian Expeditionary Forces. He served with distinction in the Ninety-Seventh battalion in France and Belgium. When the US entered the war in 1917, the battalion was transferred to General "Black Jack" Pershing's forces. Sergeant Reed was cited for bravery under fire on no less than three occasions, including a silver star when he was wounded in the Battle of Cambrai— where he was trapped in a collapsed tunnel for three days with a German soldier he'd captured.'"

A German soldier? Captured? Bone felt her eyes going as big as that ghost dog's. Uncle Junior turned to her. She just shook her head. Uncle Ash hadn't told anyone that part. The book practically vibrated in her hands.

The preacher was going on about how he too had run off to join up with the Expeditionary in the Great War. "Maybe we served in some of the same trenches, saw some of the same horrors." The preacher shivered. "What I saw made me turn to ministering to suffering souls. Sergeant Ash Reed, I think, turned to ministering to suffering animals. Each of us was changed by that awful war. May Sergeant Reed know some peace now."

"Amen."

Bone felt oddly steadier knowing that the new preacher

understood Uncle Ash, even if they'd never met. Maybe some folks would shut up about the war changing him like it was a bad thing.

During one last hymn, Bone couldn't help thinking of herself, Ash, and Corolla singing along with a song on the radio, trying to out-awful one another. The tears came, and Uncle Junior put a wiry arm around her while Mamaw patted her hair. Bone wiped her tears on her sleeve. Why was she crying? It wasn't Uncle Ash in that coffin. She couldn't help herself, though. What if it were him? Why'd he have to go away? She was so tired of people all the time leaving her behind.

The church filed out, a warm mass of sniffling people buoying Bone and her family along into the crisp wintery air. She could breathe again.

Outside, Aunt Queenie, Oscar Fears, Poppy, and about twenty other folks from Sherman's Forest stood in their Sunday best wiping their eyes. The men took off their hats as Mamaw hugged Queenie.

"Why didn't y'all come in?" Mamaw asked her.

Queenie nodded toward the sheriff leaning against his patrol car.

"Alfred, why in the world would you keep my son's friends from his funeral?"

"Some folks thought there'd be trouble on account of Tiny being arrested for Ash's death." The sheriff nodded in Mr. Matthews and Aunt Mattie's direction.

"No one in this family is stupid enough to think Tiny is responsible for that."

No one except Aunt Mattie. She probably told the sheriff to do this. Bone turned to glare at her again. She wouldn't meet Bone's eye.

Aunt Mattie didn't deserve a truce.

Mr. Matthews pushed his way through the crowd. The new preacher wasn't far behind.

"I asked the sheriff to—," Mr. Matthews started to say. "Mrs. Albert and her family have been through enough and shouldn't have to deal with—" He stopped himself and then plastered on a smile. "The kin of the man accused of murdering her brother."

"Hold on now," the new preacher interrupted. He rounded on the mine superintendent. "Everyone is welcome in this church. Everyone."

"Well, I might have to start coming to church, then," Mamaw said to no one in particular.

Mr. Matthews was not about to shut up, though, and Aunt Mattie was at his shoulder. "Mr. Stewart, there's something you need to understand—"

Several other white folks jumped into the argument.

The sheriff threw up his hands and turned to Queenie. "I think y'all better leave now before you cause any more trouble."

Aunt Queenie crossed her arms and stood her ground. Mamaw and the new preacher joined her. "All we want to do is pay our respects."

"Al, let them go in now." Uncle Junior stepped into the fray. "Ash wouldn't have wanted all this fuss on his account."

"That boy killed your brother!" someone yelled from the back of the crowd.

"He did no such thing!" someone else shouted.

"It's not him!" Bone cried out, exasperated, but her voice was lost in the din of voices. She suddenly found herself surrounded by Will, Ruby, and the boys.

"Let's get out of here," Ruby whispered.

Bone nodded.

"This could get ugly," Jake added, motioning to the crowd.

Will dug out a nickel.

"The pop's on Will," Clay said.

As they walked up to the road to the store, Bone heard the familiar rattle of a truck coming up the road from the river. She turned to see a faded yellow 1928 Chevy pickup puttering toward them. The world began to swirl again. She blinked hard several times to make sure she was seeing what she was seeing. The adults were all busy yelling at Mr. Matthews or Queenie or the new preacher or Mamaw and Uncle Junior.

"Is that . . . ?" Ruby grabbed Bone's arm, her fingernails digging into her skin.

The truck stopped at the boardinghouse—and then started up the road toward them.

"Yes!" Bone took off running as the truck pulled to a stop

in front of the church. Ruby, Will, and the boys weren't far behind her.

"Well, I'll be jiggered!" Clay exclaimed.

"Hot damn!" Jake added.

The crowd at the church parted and gawped as Uncle Ash eased himself out of the driver's side.

Corolla hung his head out the passenger's side and yipped. Kiawah and Kitty Hawk stood, front paws on the sides of the truck bed.

There was the truck. There were the dogs. And there was her Uncle Ash. Not dead.

At his own funeral.

"What are y'all doing up here?" he called.

He managed to pull a Lucky Strike out of the packet before Bone tackled him to the ground.

"Whoa, there, Forever Girl," Uncle Ash sputtered as Bone pinned him down. The dogs barked and tried to join in the roughhousing. "Everybody off," Ash commanded. The dogs obliged, and Bone rolled onto her back laughing. It was the best she'd ever felt. "I told you I'd be back before Christmas," he said, picking up the crumpled cigarette. "And I brought you a present!" He motioned toward the passenger's side of the truck.

The door swung open, and Miss Spencer stepped out.

Will reached a hand down to help Uncle Ash to his feet. Ruby pulled Bone up—and then hugged Uncle Ash quick and tight.

No sooner had Ruby let go than Aunt Mattie came steaming down the hill toward Uncle Ash. She wiped her eyes on her coat sleeve, reared back, and walloped him with her good Sunday-go-to-meeting handbag. It about knocked him off his feet again. She turned on her heel and marched toward the boardinghouse.

Uncle Junior was on his knees, his head in his hands. Bone couldn't tell if he was laughing or crying—or both.

"What the hell is going on around here?" Ash demanded as he yanked Junior to his feet.

Junior first hugged Ash and then slapped him on the back. Hard. "This is your funeral, little brother."

Uncle Ash dropped his Lucky Strike again.

Mamaw whirled around, pointing her finger at the sheriff. "I told you it weren't him."

The sheriff hung his head. "I'm glad you were right, Mrs. Reed." He looked up at Uncle Ash. "I still got some questions for you!"

Bone had to admit she did, too. Like who was that man they were fixing to bury.

15

BACK AT THE BOARDINGHOUSE, Mrs. Price plied Ash and Miss Spencer with funeral food and coffee as everyone filled them in on what had happened. About the body in the mine. About Tiny getting arrested.

"What?" Uncle Ash leapt to his feet upon hearing that last part. "We got to get him out."

Uncle Junior calmed him down. "Al must've let him go by now."

Bone nodded. As the crowd had politely let the family shoo Uncle Ash and Miss Spencer away from his own funeral, Bone had spied Aunt Queenie cornering the sheriff. Surely, he couldn't hold Mr. Sherman in jail for killing Uncle Ash when he was clearly very much alive.

Uncle Ash sank back down beside Miss Spencer.

Aunt Mattie was curiously silent as she sipped hot coffee perched on the settee, handbag by her side.

"I told them you go to the beach every year," Bone said quietly. "I know it's supposed to be a secret." She felt bad for betraying him, not so much for telling this on him but for doubting him for even a second.

"Oh, that's all right, Forever Girl." He took Miss Spencer's hand in his. "Why would anyone think that body in the mine was me?" He looked at his brother. "You know what happened last time I went down the mines."

"Yes, I told them," Junior said.

Bone and Mamaw both nodded. They'd told everyone who'd listen Ash would've never gone down there—on his own accord, at least.

Uncle Ash threw up his hands. "Then why?"

Bone opened up his poetry book, revealing the dog tag with a little bit of leather cord.

Uncle Ash raised his eyebrow as he took the tag. He read it. He turned it over in his palm again and again. Then he pulled out a matching disk that hung around his neck on a similar leather cord. They were identical. Yet there was, just like Bone remembered, a larger, more oval disk attached to the same cord. He stared at both for the longest time, going a bit white. His hand started to shake.

"Well?" Mattie demanded. She set her coffee cup down with a clatter.

"I can see why you thought it was me," he finally said, tucking his own dog tags back into his shirt.

Then it all made sense to Bone. "You gave one of your tags to someone!"

Everyone stared at her—and then at Ash and back at Bone.

That someone wore the tag after the tunnel collapsed on him. And then the tag showed another person's life. Someone who lived in the beautiful stone city nestled in snowcapped mountains. Someone who had a wife and children and strange black dogs. Someone who fought in the desert, in a tank maybe. "The German?" she added in a whisper. She could see a man wrapping the book in brown paper.

Uncle Ash turned even whiter. He looked from her to the tag back to her, figuring out what she'd seen. "I told you to never touch these."

Mamaw gave Mrs. Price a look, and she shooed Miss Johnson and Miss Spencer into the kitchen for pie. "Family business," she said by way of explanation. "We'll get some more coffee."

Bone took a deep breath. "I had to know it wasn't you."

"I asked her," Uncle Junior admitted. "I shouldn't have."

Aunt Mattie gawped from brother to brother, her gaze settling on Bone, but she didn't say anything. Her eyes bored into Bone just like they had right before she'd tried to baptize the Gift out of her. Bone could taste the iron-cold bathwater again.

"Ah, Forever Girl." Uncle Ash squeezed Bone's hand.

"But it was you—and it wasn't." Bone glanced at Aunt Mattie.

115

Her eyes narrowed into slits. "Um, the images were all jumbled up. And I couldn't figure it out," Bone explained. "Then the new preacher said you'd captured a German soldier in the tunnel."

"Beck," Uncle Ash pulled out the oval disk tied to the leather strap. "Sergeant Rainer Beck. We were trapped in that tunnel together. He wasn't my prisoner, though."

Aunt Mattie harrumphed as she picked up her coffee cup again. Mamaw shushed her.

Uncle Ash quietly explained how they'd both gotten trapped in a mortar barrage. He'd been running messages with the dogs near the German line—and Beck had been doing some scouting along Allied lines. Ash dove into the tunnel, pulling the dogs after him, only to find Beck already there, hurt. Bad. Then the tunnel collapsed. "We were both cut off from our platoons." Uncle Ash's voice was steady but his hand shook so much he couldn't light his smoke. He pitched it in the fireplace and started pacing as he talked.

"How'd you get out?" Ruby asked.

Aunt Mattie sipped her coffee, watching her brother wear a hole in the carpet; her hand shook too as she held the cup.

Ash smiled. "The dogs, of course. One of them at least. The other didn't make it. Ghost was this lovely gray Alsatian. She looked muddy-brown in the trenches. She helped me and Beck dig out just enough for her to squeeze through and run a message back to my platoon."

Mattie slammed down her cup, this time cracking the saucer.

"That was a German soldier down in Big Vein?"

"Appears so." Ash tucked his and Beck's dog tags back into his flannel shirt. He slipped the other one, the one found on Beck's body, into his pocket.

"What happened to Beck?" Bone asked, ignoring Mattie's glare.

"My people found us before his did. We were both taken to the army field hospital. He and I exchanged tags. I went back to the lines, and he went to a POW camp, I think." He lit another Lucky Strike, this time without shaking. "I sure could use some of that pie and coffee."

"Hold on a cotton-picking minute!" Aunt Mattie jumped to her feet. "There was a German soldier in Big Vein. The same Germans who killed my Henry?" She trembled with rage as she glowered at Uncle Ash. "And you knew him! How could you put me through all this? Again! Henry just died!"

"Mattie, honey." Mamaw gently took Aunt Mattie's arm, but she wasn't having it. Mattie broke away and stepped in front of Uncle Ash.

"It was a different war, Mattie," Uncle Ash told his sister. He didn't look at her, though. "A long time ago," he added softly.

Miss Spencer appeared by Uncle Ash's side and quietly took his hand, intertwining her fingers with his.

Aunt Mattie stiffened and stalked past them, out through the kitchen, slamming the screen door after her. Ruby sprang up and started to follow her mother out. She dashed back to hug

Uncle Ash and then she was out the door, too.

It was little wonder Aunt Mattie was furious. She'd almost buried a German soldier. In Big Vein. Near Uncle Henry. There was a bigger mystery at work here than anybody had suspected. But right now, Bone didn't care. Uncle Ash was home—and he wasn't dead.

Mrs. Price and Miss Johnson came bustling in with fresh coffee and pecan pie.

It was the best damn pie Bone ever tasted.

16

BONE'S PIE-FILLED HAPPINESS lasted well into the evening. Miss Spencer told everyone how Uncle Ash surprised her at the college, just as she was editing the final draft of the stories she'd collected.

"I stayed at the motor court near the college," Uncle Ash answered Mrs. Price's disapproving glare. "Anyways, several of the filling stations in Roanoke were low on fuel, so I figured I might not have enough gas to get all the way to the Outer Banks this year."

"Well, I'm glad you didn't chance it." Mamaw downed the last of her coffee as she rose. "I knew it weren't you." She leaned over to kiss Ash on the forehead. "And you ended up just where you needed to be." She winked at Miss Spencer. "Now, I best go check on your sister." Mamaw gathered up her empty plate and fork and disappeared into the kitchen and out the back door.

The radio played the war news while everyone else had another slice of pie. The CBS radioman, Mr. Murrow, was talking about how the Germans were killing millions of Jews. *Millions? How could that be*, Bone wondered.

Uncle Ash worried the dog tag, rolling it around in his hand. Bone caught him looking at her once or twice. Then he stuffed the tag back in his pocket. Uncle Junior got out their war map and marked a battle in Tunisia where the German tanks had retreated.

～

The sheriff knocked on the door about 8:30 in the evening.

"So, Ash, why did this fellow have nothing but your dog tag on him?" the sheriff asked over a slice of pie.

"Nothing?" Ash asked, his eyebrow climbing.

"You know what I mean." He stuffed the last bite in his mouth and waited. "Who was he? And how'd he get down there?"

Uncle Ash stood up and fished out a pack of Luckies from his shirt pocket. He offered one to the sheriff, who stuck it behind his ear, and gulped down black coffee. Ash took his time lighting his, but not taking his eye off the sheriff either, like he was deciding what to tell him. "Rainer Beck. I don't know how in the world he got here or who would kill him." Uncle Ash took out his own dog tags. He showed the sheriff both the matching dog tag and the tarnished disk that said RAINER BECK across the top. The other two lines, Ash explained, were the infantry unit and identification numbers.

The sheriff peered at the tags, leaning back in his seat, clearly puzzled.

"I saved his life—and he kept me sane—in that tunnel." Uncle Ash tucked his tags back into his shirt. Ash explained what had happened during the war.

"We ran into those tunnels at the Somme in '18." The sheriff shook his head. "Nasty business." Uncle Ash and the sheriff compared notes on their war experience. The Brits, French, and Germans had dug tunnels throughout France and Belgium trying to get at each other. They even put explosives in the tunnels, killing hundreds, if not thousands, of men when they blew.

"When was the last time you saw the Jerrie?" The sheriff pulled out a little notebook and jotted down the name.

"December 8, 1917, in a field hospital in Cambrai, France." Uncle Ash flicked his cigarette butt into the fireplace. "He was being taken to a POW camp."

"So you exchanged tags?"

"Yep."

"And *that's* the last you saw him?"

"Yep."

The sheriff scratched his head. "So where have you been?"

"I started off for the shore as usual this time a year." Uncle Ash stopped to light a smoke, his hand shaking.

The sheriff flicked through his notebook. "Cambrai was about now, right?"

"Yes." Uncle Ash shivered ever so slightly. "The first snap of cold brings it back . . . I head to where it's a bit warmer." Uncle Ash glanced at Miss Spencer with a smile. "But I only got as far as Roanoke this time."

Miss Spencer stood and took Uncle Ash's hand. "I can vouch for his whereabouts."

Uncle Ash made the introductions, explaining that she was a professor at the women's college. "We drove back this morning."

"The faculty Christmas party was last night," she added.

Bone stifled a giggle. She couldn't imagine Uncle Ash at a party with a bunch of college professors.

"Your uncle charmed my dean quite nicely," Miss Spencer told Bone.

"Where were you last Saturday night?" the sheriff asked Ash.

"Let's see, I was in Whitethorne birthing Sy Long's calf until late into the wee hours. It got stuck. Him and Cassie fed me breakfast after."

That's exactly what she'd seen.

"This case makes less and less sense every minute. Maybe this fella Beck moved to the States after the first war. My cousin Adele's husband's family did. But that still don't explain how he got into shaft twenty-seven. Dead." The sheriff shook Uncle Ash's hand as he was headed out the door. "Glad it wasn't you, Ash, but somehow you're involved in this. Don't go nowhere."

"It wasn't me—or Tiny. You let Tiny go, right?" Uncle Ash asked.

The sheriff shook his head.

"Al, you know Tiny didn't kill Beck." Uncle Ash squared up with the sheriff.

Uncle Junior laid a quiet hand on his brother's shoulder. Ash shrugged it off.

"Some evidence still points to him," the sheriff replied, looking Uncle Ash in the eye.

The ball cap.

"But he could've easily left his cap when he was working in the shaft," Junior said.

"Yeah, but someone was stealing coal—and I still got a body."

"Tiny ain't responsible for either." Ash crossed his arms.

Somebody attacked that German man under the tipple and dragged him down into Big Vein to die.

And there was the ghost dog. Bone didn't think the sheriff wanted to hear about it. Uncle Ash would, though.

17

COME MONDAY MORNING, practically the whole seventh grade was waiting to walk Bone and Ruby to school. Even Robbie Matthews was there, standing in the road with his sack lunch and books. Bone suspected, though, he was more interested in impressing Ruby than hearing about Uncle Ash.

"Well?" Jake asked after they'd passed the parsonage.

"Well what?" Bone pretended not to know what he was talking about.

"What did the sheriff say last night?" Clay prodded. Everyone knew everyone's business in Big Vein.

"Yeah, whose body was that we almost buried yesterday?" Jake asked.

Bone hesitated. She'd almost blurted it out, but Ruby

raised an eyebrow and ever so slightly tilted her head toward Robbie. Bone trusted Jake and Clay—and maybe even the Little Jewels—but not the son of the mine superintendent. And Robbie Matthews was all ears.

Loose Lips Might Sink Ships, the war poster in the store said. They'd already had too many sunk ships.

Bone shrugged. "The sheriff just wanted to know where Uncle Ash was."

Clay started to say something but Jake punched him, nodding toward Robbie. He was oblivious.

"Father always said it was a bum off the train. Knew it as soon as the call came, he said," Robbie relayed with great assurance. "I brought something to show you," he told Ruby, patting his coat pocket.

Ruby rolled her eyes, but only so Bone could see it.

Jake and Clay moved the conversation along to football. The Little Jewels talked about the dance.

Bone's breath hung cloud-like in the crisp, still air as she walked. Did Rainer Beck move to the States, like the sheriff thought? With his family and those black dogs? The mountains and town didn't look like anything she'd seen. But she hadn't seen a lot. Was he coming to see Uncle Ash? Who would kill him? Was it on account of him being German? Another reason not to say anything about it.

These thoughts haunted Bone throughout the morning.

School wore on, meandering through history, math, and

geography, all like nothing happened last week, like there was no German soldier murdered two hundred feet from the school. Like they hadn't seen a ghost dog hovering over that very spot.

Bone leaned back in her chair and whispered to the boys, "We need to go back to the tipple at night—and take Uncle Ash with us."

"Hot damn," Jake whispered back.

Clay nodded solemnly. "Then you can tell us who really got himself killed there."

Bone didn't answer.

"Then you owe us another devil dog story at lunch," Jake said.

"Deal," Bone agreed. She'd fill them and Will in later when she had more of the picture.

"Would you three like to clean the erasers after school?" Miss Johnson appeared in front of them.

"No ma'am," they said in unison.

At lunch, Bone told the boys—and most of the fifth, sixth, and seventh grades—another ghost dog tale. "Many years ago, a man followed his wife up the road to a great sycamore tree," Bone began. "She was meeting another fella there. The husband killed them both on the spot. Fifty years later, a man and a couple of ladies were walking up that road on the way to a church social. Pretty soon, they saw a big black dog was a-following them. It had eyes of burning coal." Bone paused for effect.

Most of the class had their eyes on Bone—except Robbie Matthews. He was pulling something out of his pocket to show Ruby.

"Well?" Jake asked.

Clay nodded. "You just love leaving us in the dark."

"The man threw a rock at the dog—and the rock went clean through it. They started walking right fast up the road toward the church, hoping to lose it. As soon as they passed that sycamore tree, the dog disappeared into thin air. Plum on the spot those two people died."

Jake and Clay exchanged a look. One of the other kids oohed.

Robbie, though, was showing Ruby something, a military medal.

Or was it a dog tag?

⁓

"What you got there?" Bone asked Robbie as they filed back into the schoolroom.

He clutched an old cigar box to his chest. "Some of Daddy's souvenirs from the war." He turned to her. "Wanna see?"

Bone nodded. She motioned him toward her and the boys' seats at the back of the room. Jake, Clay, and Ruby followed.

Robbie set up shop at Bone's desk. He opened the battered cigar box, lifting the lid slowly to reveal its treasures. Inside lay medals, some with little ribbons, some with dangling crosses or stars. Some were simple silver disks—not dog tags as Bone had thought. He picked one up gingerly. "Daddy won this for bravery at the Somme." That medal had a star on it. He picked up another one, this time with a black cross. "Daddy took this off a Kraut he killed." Robbie laid out a few more as he described an epic battle in which his father was the hero.

Bone's hand brushed against the cigar box as she reached for a medal. She saw Robbie, with the box tucked under his arm, sneak into a big room full of bookshelves and glass cases. His daddy's study. He made a beeline for the big wooden desk at one end and plopped down in the leather chair. Robbie twirled around in it once, quickly stopping it when papers on the desk went flying. He scrambled to pick them up, many of them stamped FINAL NOTICE. Robbie selected one of Mr. Matthews's cigars. He rolled it between his thumb and forefinger, smelling the tobacco, just like he'd seen his daddy do many times. Sticking the cigar in his mouth, careful not to leave any marks, though, Robbie sidled over to a row of glass cases. In one, several baseball caps were lined up. The Grays. The Black Barons. The Stars. Dust outlined a missing cap. Over them hung a signed bat. Robbie moved on to the next case. Inside it, there were more medals, dog tags, knives, guns, and other war trinkets than Bone could count. Robbie lifted up the glass, picked out a medal, and told himself a story about it. It was the same one Robbie was telling now about a completely different medal.

Did Mr. Matthews tell him that story? The scene shifted. Robbie sat at a long wooden table, a plate of roast beef and potatoes in front of him. His parents sat on opposite ends, his father walled off behind the newspaper. *"Father, I got an A on the math test."*

Mr. Matthews snapped the paper closed and folded it in half. *"I'm going to Greensboro tomorrow,"* he told Mrs. Matthews. He didn't even look at Robbie.

"It's such a shame about Norton's car dealership," Mrs. Matthews replied. She tsked-tsked as she cut into her meat. *"The war effort takes its toll on us all."*

"We're exploring other opportunities," Mr. Matthews told his wife.

❧

"Bone." Ruby nudged her. "Robbie asked if Uncle Ash has any medals."

Bone shook herself. Robbie's dad barely acknowledged he existed. Robbie told himself those stories. She felt sorry for him—until she saw the sneer on his upper lip as he waited for Bone's answer.

"Yes, but Uncle Ash don't like to brag," Bone finally said. He didn't. It wasn't until his so-called funeral that anyone in the family ever heard he'd won a silver star.

"He's got nothing to brag about," Robbie said as he brushed the medals back into his cigar box. Looking up at Ruby's best Aunt Mattie–like glare, he muttered, "Sorry."

He clearly didn't mean it. But Bone had seen a tiny glimpse of what made him such a misery.

18

WHEN BONE GOT HOME to the boardinghouse, the kitchen smelled like Christmas dinner. Mrs. Price hummed happily as she stirred a pot of beans, a thick ham bone simmering in the middle. The aroma was more pork than beans. A batch of her cinnamon and molasses cookies cooled on the counter. Fresh-cut pine boughs, cones, and holly lay on the kitchen table. Mrs. Price always made a wreath for the front door and decorated the mantel in the parlor. And Daddy usually cut a nice tree for the parlor.

Only he wasn't going to be here this year. "Maybe me and Uncle Ash can go fetch a tree after supper." Bone swiped a cookie from the tray. Mrs. Price didn't mind one bit.

"That would be lovely." Mrs. Price pulled a whole chicken out of the icebox. "Why don't you get the decorations from the attic?" She began neatly and efficiently thwacking the bird into parts with her butcher knife—all while humming "God Rest Ye Merry Gentlemen."

Even from the attic, Bone could smell the chicken frying. The box of decorations was kept in a place of honor by the big window. Most of them were Daddy and Mama's, some were Mrs. Price's, and others belonged to other tenants over the years. Many of the ornaments were handmade—little wooden rocking horses, bells, and nutcrackers Papaw had carved.

Bone's favorite, though, was the box of Shiny Brite glass ornaments Mama had bought at the five-and-dime store in town. Bone traced her finger around the faded green Christmas tree with red ornaments drawn on the lid. Through cutouts in the cardboard, you could see the real ornaments inside, all shiny and bright. Bone loved the pink-and-white one with the silver flower inset into it. She saw Mama holding up the green-and-white one shaped like a tree. She patted her protruding belly. *"Laurel, I got these for you. Next Christmas and every one after that we'll put these up together."* They did for six Christmases. Then she and Daddy put them up for six more Christmases. And now . . . and now she'd just have to do it herself.

She set the carton aside and dug around in the box, looking for the tree topper. It was Mrs. Price's, a chipped white star made out of glass. Bone saw Mr. Price lifting up a boy to put the star on the top of a tree decorated with candles and twinkling ornaments. Mrs. Price then lovingly wrapped the star and other ornaments in newspaper, happy but sad Christmas was over.

The star was the only one of those twinkly ornaments left. And Mr. Price and the son were gone. Bone carefully wrapped the star and placed it and Mama's ornaments back in the cardboard box.

A door jangled and slammed downstairs. Boots stomped up the steps to the floor below—and another door slammed. By the time Bone returned to the kitchen with the box, Mrs. Price was no longer humming.

"What was that ruckus?" Bone asked.

"Heck if I know." Mrs. Price decapitated a carrot with a whack.

⁓

Supper was uncommonly quiet, almost like Uncle Ash really did die. It was just Bone, Uncle Junior, and Mrs. Price—and Uncle Junior wasn't talking. He pushed around his food, his mind a million miles away. Mrs. Price collected his full plate and stormed into the kitchen. He didn't say anything until Bone polished off her chicken and was sopping up the gravy with her second biscuit.

"Bone, honey, you didn't say anything about that German fella, did you?"

Bone shook her head. Loose lips might sink ships.

"Good. Don't." And that's all he'd say about it. He pushed himself up from the table wearily and dragged himself into the parlor. The radio clicked on to the *Lum and Abner* show.

Bone cleared the rest of the dishes and brought them to Mrs. Price.

"What in tarnation is his problem tonight?" Mrs. Price said in a low voice.

"Heck if I know," Bone answered. She really didn't. He'd been so happy when Uncle Ash turned up not dead.

"Well aren't we a pair?" Mrs. Price handed Bone a dish towel.

Mrs. Price proceeded to wash the dishes without humming, handing each to Bone to dry. Bone told her about school and about Robbie asking Ruby to the Christmas dance.

"You and Will are going, aren't you?" Mrs. Price perked up.

Bone shrugged. She didn't much care for dances. But Mrs. Price was humming again. The fact was, though, that Will hadn't asked her. Yet.

"I'll make you a new dress—well, not new exactly." Mrs. Price was a wizard with her sewing machine. She'd made Bone several feedsack dresses for the school year—but Aunt Mattie had donated them to the needy. "There must be a dress of Willow's still up in the attic." She'd also made Bone her Sunday dresses out of some of Mama's old ones. "Anyway, you'll have a far handsomer and kinder date than Robbie Matthews. The apple doesn't fall far from the tree."

The knock came at the usual time.

"Speak of the devil." Mrs. Price turned off the spigot and took the dish towel back from Bone. "Ya'll help yourself to some pie and milk," she told Will as he stepped into the kitchen. "It's about time for my program." With that, she hummed herself into the parlor.

Bone poured two glasses of milk, and Will cut two slices of pie. On top of all the food Mrs. Price just fixed, they still had plenty of funeral food left. Were you supposed to give it back if the funeral was a bit premature?

"How was work today?" Bone asked as she sunk her fork into the gooey pie. She was beginning to tire of pecan pie, if that was possible.

"Odd!" Will gulped down half his milk and then started writing.

"Why aren't you talking?" she whispered.

He nodded toward the parlor—and Uncle Junior.

Mr. Matthews came down the mine!

"Why ever for?" He never went into Big Vein, at least that's what the boys had said.

Will shrugged. *He and Junior went down to 27.*

That was odd.

"When Junior got back, he was steamed," Will whispered. *Told me not to mention the German.*

"Me, too. Just now." Bone had a bad feeling about this. That meeting with Mr. Matthews had put Uncle Junior in his foul Christmas-spirit-killing mood.

Army contract.

She took the pad and pencil from Will and wrote: *One of Mr. Matthews's deals.*

They'd both seen Mr. Matthews muscle Uncle Junior into doing things his way.

Will nodded. Mr. Matthews didn't want the army to know they'd found a dead German guy in Big Vein. That would certainly make it hard to meet the quota with the brass sniffing around and maybe shutting down the mine. Big Vein might even lose the contract.

No one would ever find out who killed Rainer Beck—and his family might never know what happened to him.

"That's not right," Bone said.

Will nodded. "But I need my job."

So did Uncle Junior and every other family in Big Vein. Daddy would need his, too, when he came back from the army.

But it still wasn't right. Somebody needed to hear Beck's story—even it if was only Bone. And Uncle Ash.

Did Uncle Junior tell him and Mamaw about the meeting? Is that why they weren't there for dinner?

Let's go back to the tipple tomorrow night, Bone wrote.

With Ash? Will wrote.

"Yes, he at least needs to see that ghost dog."

Will nodded as he licked the pie crumbs from the plate.

19

AFTER SCHOOL, BONE STOPPED BY the Scott Brothers' store to pick up the sugar ration for Mrs. Price. When Bone emerged, the yellow pickup was parked out front—but no Ash or Miss Spencer. Bone put her hand on the still-warm hood. Among the scenes she'd felt before, Bone saw Uncle Ash and Miss Spencer sitting on the hood, leaning against the windshield, under a starry sky. The truck was parked next to a dark lake or pond, its waters gently lapping against the shore. The dogs snored in the bed of the truck while the humans talked into the night.

It was so peaceful.

Up the road, a dog growled and whined. It was Corolla. Kiawah and Kitty Hawk popped their heads up from the truck bed. Uncle Ash and Miss Spencer were walking near the tipple.

Corolla stopped and snapped at something unseen, and then started slowly backing away, the hair on his shoulders bristling, tail low. The hounds ran to the little dog—and then started slinking backward, too, and whimpering. Bone followed.

"What in the Sam Hill is wrong with you dogs?" Uncle Ash asked. He kicked at the very spot the ghost dog had stood. The dogs kept backing away, the big dogs skulking behind little Corolla.

"Back to the truck," Bone told the dogs. They turned tail and ran to the safety of the yellow pickup. She bent down to hold her hand over the spot. She couldn't feel anything. The coal that had landed on Beck was probably halfway to Norfolk by now. Or burned up in someone's furnace. Bone stood and looked her uncle in the eye.

"There's something you need to see. Tonight after supper. Don't bring the dogs."

Uncle Ash looked both amused and bewildered. "Can I bring a date?"

"Dress warm," she told Miss Spencer with a wink.

⁓⁓

Supper was quiet again—even with Uncle Ash and Miss Spencer there. Miss Spencer and Miss Johnson carried the conversation, talking about the goings-on back at the college. The brothers avoided talking to each other during most of the meal.

Finally, Uncle Ash spoke. "I went to see Tiny."

Junior looked up from pushing his green beans around the plate. "Did Al drop the charges?"

"Nope. I got him to deputize a few more people to watch the jail, just in case . . ." Uncle Ash lit a cigarette. His plate was as untouched as Junior's. "You know what? That weren't even Tiny's cap. Queenie found his right where he left it on his dresser. Al claims Tiny must've had two, and there's other evidence besides. Leave it to lawyers, he said. But no one will represent Tiny, leastwise not around here."

A thought hit Bone. Was the missing cap in Mr. Matthew's study a Memphis Red Sox one? The Grays. The Black Barons. The Stars. Those were the other caps. Were they Negro league teams, too? She'd never heard Will and the boys mention those teams or heard their games played on the radio. Why would a man like Mr. Matthews—who obviously didn't like black people—collect them? The man was a puzzlement.

"That poor man hasn't got a lawyer?" Mrs. Price asked as she brought in the pecan pie.

"I thought everyone got one when they're arrested," Bone said. In every detective novel or movie she'd seen, the criminal always got some guy in a suit to speak for him or her. But then again, they were all white in those movies.

"Technically, everyone is entitled to a fair and speedy trial as well as an attorney, under the Constitution," Miss Spencer replied.

Uncle Ash shook his head. "But the judge can't make someone

139

take a client if he don't want to. And the white lawyers don't want to." He tamped out his cigarette in the ashtray—under Mrs. Price's glare—and took a piece of pie from her. "So Oscar ran over to Radford to talk to the NAACP last week."

"Who are they?" Bone asked. Uncle Junior's and Mrs. Price's faces were blank.

"The National Association for the Advancement of Colored People," Miss Spencer explained. "They work for civil rights."

"They're calling in someone from Richmond to take Tiny's case." Uncle Ash dug into his pecan pie.

"Oliver Hill," Miss Spencer added. "He used to practice in Roanoke. Now he works on big cases for the NAACP. He got the black teachers in Norfolk equal pay!"

"He won't be here for another day or two," Uncle Ash said through a mouthful of pecans. "He's wrapping up some lawsuit in Sussex first."

"Let's hope he can handle a murder case," Junior said. "And that certain white folks don't go after Tiny or his new lawyer."

"And that justice is color-blind." Uncle Ash refilled his coffee. "You know they won't put any black folks on that jury."

The grown-ups fell silent at that. Mr. Hill, Bone realized, must be black, too. Both him and Mr. Sherman were still in danger despite Tiny being obviously innocent. Plus there was no telling whether the Richmond lawyer could win the case with a white jury deciding Tiny's fate. Bone pushed away her pie.

Uncle Junior cleared his throat. "You didn't mention the German to anyone, did you?"

Uncle Ash set his cup down with a clatter. "I did not." He looked squarely at his brother.

Uncle Junior started to say something.

"I understand, Junior," Uncle Ash cut him off. "It's not your fault, but I don't have to like it."

Uncle Junior had obviously told Ash not to say anything about the German. Bone understood why. Mr. Matthews didn't want to risk the army contract, and Uncle Junior certainly didn't want to risk everyone's jobs. But how could the lawyer defend Tiny if neither of them knew whom he supposedly killed? This was worse than a bad Charlie Chan movie.

Uncle Junior turned his attention back to the pecan pie—as did everyone else.

Uncle Ash lit two cigarettes and passed one to Miss Spencer. "I hear you got to ride with Mamaw up the mountain," he said to Bone, obviously ready to talk about happier things.

"It takes far less time to get there when she drives." Bone actually liked the feeling of racing up the mountain. Coming down, though, she'd gotten a bit green around the gills.

"Now you know why I don't let her drive my truck." Uncle Ash laughed.

"Is your mother a bad driver?" Miss Spencer asked.

"No. The poor truck couldn't take it." Uncle Ash shook

his head. "She drove shine better than me or Daddy."

Bone laughed. "You mean faster!" She mimicked herself holding on to the door handle for dear life.

Junior laughed, too. "I'd forgot all about that."

Mrs. Price came into the dining room with more coffee. "Now that's what I like at my table, laughter—and clean plates."

~ ⁊ ~

The knock on the screen door came at the usual time. Only this time, Will had company. Jake, Clay, and Ruby. Ruby wore britches, but she still brought a blanket and thermos.

Uncle Ash and Miss Spencer exchanged a worried look as they all set off up the road.

"Bone?" he asked.

"Trust me," Bone said.

"How do we know it'll be there tonight?" Ruby asked.

"Yeah, maybe it only shows up on that night?" Clay said.

"And time," Jake added.

Will tapped his watch and shone his flashlight on it. Nearly 8:00 p.m. "I saw it last night. After the 8:15," Will said.

"It?" Miss Spencer asked.

"Saw what?" Uncle Ash was getting a bit exasperated.

Ruby giggled. The boys had big grins on their faces.

Uncle Ash deserved a little razzing considering what they'd all been through.

Just as they reached the edge of Flat Woods, Bone turned the flashlight to light up her own face for effect. "The ghost dog."

Uncle Ash stopped in his tracks.

"Come on." Bone shone the light into the woods.

"You're not afraid of a little ghost, are you?" Jake teased.

"Well, I am," Clay answered. "Just about wet my pants last time." He shook it off and marched into Flat Woods with Jake and Will.

Miss Spencer took Uncle Ash's arm. "I thought those were just stories."

Uncle Ash shook his head. "Lead on," he told Bone.

They followed the same track as before. Bone quietly explained what they'd seen on Saturday night—and what Mr. Childress had said afterward. Soon Ruby was spreading out the blanket over the same spot.

The 8:15 train came and its cars filled with coal.

Will fidgeted. Just as the last of the coal poured into the last car, Will slipped a piece of paper into Bone's hand.

She held the note every which way, but it was too dark to read.

"Go with me to the dance," Will whispered over the noise of the train.

Bone nodded. They were going anyway. Might as well go together.

Will held his cupped hand to his ear as if he couldn't hear her.

"Okay," she muttered, knowing she'd be drowned out by the train noise.

He cupped his hand again.

"Yes," she hissed louder.

He did it again.

"I'll go with you to the blame dance!" Bone sputtered. The train had gone, and Ruby, Jake, and Clay stifled their giggles.

Bone buried her face in the blanket.

Then the barn owl screeched and swooped down from the tipple, flying over them and into Flat Woods. When Bone looked up again, the black dog stepped out of the shadows, its saucer eyes gazing back.

Uncle Ash stood, staring at the devil dog. Its pointy ears swiveled toward them, and its saucer eyes locked onto Uncle Ash.

Bone rose beside him. "Y'all stay here," she whispered to the rest.

I brought him, she silently told the ghost dog.

Uncle Ash stepped forward, but the dog didn't disappear. It stood at attention, its stubby tail doing the same. The dog let Uncle Ash get within striking distance. Then it turned and loped toward the mine entrance—and disappeared.

"Sweet Jesus," Uncle Ash said.

"Rainer Beck was struck on this spot," Bone said. "Then he got dragged down into the mine." She pointed after the dog.

The boys, Ruby, and Miss Spencer came running from the woods.

"I've never seen a dog like that," Ruby said. "Even if it weren't a ghost."

"I have," Uncle Ash said. "It's a Doberman pinscher. A German breed. The Jerries used them in the trenches and as guard dogs."

He lit a cigarette while he stared after the dog. Bone couldn't peel herself away either.

Ruby cleared her throat. "We better get back seeing as it's a school night."

Uncle Ash nodded absently. "Go on ahead," Bone told the gang.

"Did you pee yourself this time?" Jake asked Clay—and got promptly punched in the arm.

They walked ahead with Ruby and Miss Spencer, regaling her with more devil dog stories, all of which Bone had told them.

"Sergeant Beck had two of those Dobermans, didn't he?" Bone asked Uncle Ash as they purposefully lagged behind.

"Did you see that?" Uncle Ash nodded. "He bred and raised them. Here in the States and back home in Munich."

That must have been the stone city she'd seen him in.

"He was a major last I heard from him. Before we got into this war, he was assigned to a panzer division. Tanks."

This time Bone stopped. That's what she'd seen, Beck riding in a tank in the desert—where he got captured. She'd imagined, like the sheriff did, Beck had been a civilian who moved to America years ago. A major? And he'd been fighting in the desert—against Daddy.

"Wait, do you mean this man was a Nazi?"

20

UNCLE ASH HAD SOME EXPLAINING TO DO. Not only
had Beck been fighting Daddy, but his people sunk Uncle
Henry's ship. And the radio said the Germans were killing
millions. Millions! How could Uncle Ash be friends with a Nazi?

He didn't answer right away, though, at least not until they
got to the boardinghouse. He motioned for her to sit down on the
front steps, then struck a match on the stoop and lit his Lucky.

"When we were trapped in that tunnel, we had plenty of time
to talk," he finally said, letting out a long stream of white smoke.

"Do you speak German?" Bone wrapped her arms around
her knees.

"Nah, he spoke better English than me. Beck was going to
college in Chicago when the war broke out. Then he went back

after the armistice—and marrying his childhood sweetheart—to finish his schooling. Engineering or architecture, I think. He wanted to build skyscrapers. He started writing me at Christmas every year when he was working on some big bank building in Cleveland. I got cards from New York, Chicago, Detroit, and even Toronto."

Uncle Ash sank down on the step next to her.

"How did he end up in a tank?" Bone asked. She'd figured Beck must be too old, like Uncle Ash, to get drafted.

"His family was all army. Generals and field marshals, and such. You know, the big brass. They called him and his wife and kids home before the war started in '39 and lined him up with a command in the Afrika Korps." Uncle Ash shook his head. "That's the last I heard from him. I wrote back to tell him to stay." He took another long drag on his cigarette. The exhaled smoke floated above them. "I don't excuse his going back. He coulda stayed. Greta and the boys were in the States, too. But they all moved back to Munich—"

"You told the sheriff you hadn't seen him since 1917."

"Well, I haven't *seen* him since then." He stamped out his cigarette and fieldstripped it. Then he pulled out his dog tags, both of them. They hung there, together, like they had since 1917. "Look, all I know is that he saved my life as much as I saved his."

Bone was grateful for that at least. She couldn't imagine her life without Uncle Ash. "What did y'all talk about in that tunnel?" she finally asked.

"Our homes. Dogs. And stories." Uncle Ash grinned. "He told me his favorites from the Brothers Grimm—and from Wagner. I told him plenty of Jack Tales—and spirit dog stories. He was right partial to those." He studied the German's dog tag for a moment and then tucked them both back into his shirt.

And now Beck had his own ghost dog to guard where he fell.

They sat in silence for a while, listening to the train across the river round the bend.

"So what are you going to do?" she asked Uncle Ash.

"Forever Girl, I don't rightly know." Uncle Ash lit another Lucky Strike. "If I call the army, Mr. Matthews is going to fire Junior and whoever else he likes."

Like Daddy or even Will.

"It ain't fair," Bone said. "What about Tiny?"

"That does put me in a quandary." Uncle Ash took a long drag of his smoke and let it out. "Calling the army might not help Tiny neither." He tossed the still-burning cigarette on the ground and crushed it under his boot. "They might pin a medal on Tiny. Or they might side with the sheriff and Mr. Matthews."

On one hand, Rainer Beck was the enemy, and worse, a Nazi. His people were killing millions. But Big Vein was no battlefield in Belgium—or North Africa. Someone *murdered* him. Someone who was *not* Tiny Sherman. And no one would know what happened to Beck. His family would feel like Bone's had, only worse. No one would hear his story.

Was that what her Gift wanted? To tell the story? Bone shivered.

That's what the ghost dog wanted, too. But how could she do that without risking everyone's jobs? Or Tiny's neck?

"Uncle Ash?" Bone asked slowly. "What if we solved the mystery ourselves?"

Uncle Ash looked up. "Where would we start? We don't even know how he got here."

Bone thought for a second. "He was in the army, right? Wouldn't he still have a dog tag, even if he got captured?"

"Yes!" Uncle Ash stood up, hand on his dog tags. "But the sheriff said he was only wearing mine. Oh—"

Whoever killed him took his other dog tag.

"What if we found Beck's dog tag?" Bone asked.

Uncle Ash snapped his fingers. "I can ask around a couple places in Radford. Somebody might have tried to sell it as a souvenir."

"A souvenir?" Bone had a bad feeling about this.

"Some folks collect and sell war medals, dog tags, knives, and guns. German ones are worth a lot—even during the war. I saw orderlies and soldiers strip things right off German prisoners and the dead to sell on the black market. These days, pawnshops and auction houses deal in those types of things."

Robbie's father had all those things in a glass case in his study, including dog tags. Her Gift had shown her that.

21

MRS. JOHNSON READ FROM *A Christmas Carol*, the part where stingy ole Mr. Scrooge is mean to his clerk and doesn't want to give to charity. Under the cover of her textbook, Ruby slipped the Little Jewels a picture torn from the Sears & Roebuck catalog. It was the dress she was wearing to the dance.

Bone didn't care about the dance—or the working conditions of Victorian England. She cared that Robbie Matthews actually deigned to show up today. He'd been out sick two whole days! It was Friday already, and she'd have to get a look at his souvenirs soon. Uncle Ash and Miss Spencer hadn't had any luck finding anything at the pawn shops in the whole New River Valley. Bone needed to convince Robbie to bring in the dog tags.

During math, Robbie leaned back and whispered, "Father said your uncle was no hero, not like him, of course."

Bone steamed. Miss Johnson shushed them both—even though Bone hadn't said a word. Yet.

She had a plan, though. She just needed to egg Robbie on a bit.

~⚬~

"Did I ever tell you all about the Christmas truce of 1914? It's a war story of Uncle Ash's." That got Robbie Matthews's attention—and he slid into a seat next to Jake. She told the boys and Little Jewels what Uncle Ash told her, how soldiers on both sides of the trenches stopped the war to celebrate Christmas Day—but the big brass tried to stop it. And it didn't ever happen again.

"Oh, you're making that up," Robbie complained. "Father never said anything about no Christmas truce."

"He wasn't there yet—unless he joined up early like Uncle Ash. He fought with the Canadians and Brits three whole years before your daddy even got into the war."

"But mine killed a lot of Germans! He even has the souvenirs to prove it."

"He does not!" Bone countered, beginning to feel a tiny bit bad now for egging him on.

"Real dog tags and medals plucked right off their chests!"

"Now *you're* making that up."

"I'll prove it!" Robbie sprang up. "I'll be right back. If'n she asks, tell Miss Johnson I forgot my lunch and ran home to get it." He took off running up the road past the mine toward the big house on the hill.

"That was easier than I thought," Bone whispered to herself. "I'll explain later," she told Ruby and the boys as they looked at her expectantly.

"You better!" Jake said. "All this mystery is killing me."

"And you know the price, Bone!" Clay said.

"Oh, I agree," Ruby jumped in. "You won't tell us what's going on, then you need to tell us a story."

"A good and scary one," Jake added. "But maybe not a ghost dog one."

Another story. Bone was almost getting tired of telling them. Almost.

This time she told them about the Greenbrier ghost.

"Over in West Virginia, a young newlywed named Zona died suddenly," Bone began. "Now they all thought it was natural causes—at least that's what the husband said it was. He arranged to have the body buried quick so nobody could check. The night she was buried, Zona's ghost appeared to her mother and told her the man abused her. He broke her neck because she didn't put no meat on the table. The ghost swiveled her head clean around to prove it. The next night the ghost appeared again and told the same story. And the next night. And the next."

"Ooh." Ruby squirmed but she was still all ears.

"Dang!" Jake said.

"Now, we're talking about a story!" Clay added.

"Well, Zona's mama went to the prosecutor and convinced him to dig up Zona's body. They did the autopsy right in the local school." Bone paused to look around the school yard for effect. "And sure enough, Zona's neck was broken. They arrested her husband. Her mother got up in court and told them exactly what the ghost had said—and done."

"What happened to the man?" Ruby asked.

The boys leaned in.

"He died in prison. Later it came out he'd had several wives and killed at least one other one, too," Bone concluded. "That's the only time a ghost ever helped convict her own murderer."

Could the Big Vein ghost dog help catch Beck's murderer?

Just as Miss Johnson rang the bell, Robbie came chugging back down the road like a winded steam engine. He spread out a number of dog tags of varying sizes. None of them looked exactly like the one Ash wore around his neck. Most had names on them. Krieg. Stollen. Schmidt. No Beck. One of the tags was bigger and shinier. A deep line split it down the middle, with the same thing stamped on the top and bottom halves. No name. It was mostly numbers with a few letters Bone didn't understand. She brushed it aside to look at the others. A flash of surprise and pain assaulted her. Trying not to flinch, Bone picked up the bigger tag again. In it, she saw the same woman and children, now older, young men almost. And the same black dogs.

Robbie snatched the tag from her hand. "Don't smudge

them." He wiped it with his sleeve and laid it out carefully on the table. "See, I didn't make it up."

The son didn't but his daddy might have. He hadn't got all those tags during the Great War.

The odd one belonged to Beck, she was sure of it. But it didn't have a name. Bone tried to commit those numbers and letters to memory. She reached for it again. "You're right, Robbie. And you know who'd love to see these? Will—and my uncle. Could I take one to show him?"

Robbie swept up the tags. "No, Daddy will miss . . . I mean, he doesn't like me to lend them out. Too valuable, you know."

Mr. Matthews clearly didn't know Robbie took his war trinkets. How was she going to get time to read this one—away from Robbie—and show it to Uncle Ash?

The dance.

"Bring them tomorrow night," Bone finally said. "Everyone will be there."

"Deal!" Robbie grinned. He poured the tags back into his pockets. "Maybe I'll bring some medals, too." He sauntered back into the schoolhouse.

"You got a pencil?" Bone took one from Jake's shirt pocket, tore off a piece of brown paper from her lunch poke, and scribbled down the numbers she could remember.

Jake and Clay peered over her shoulder. "Maybe we ought to go to this dance, too," Jake said.

Clay nodded vigorously. "And then maybe you'll tell us what's going on!"

"Maybe," Bone said with a grin. "Come by tonight after supper."

Miss Johnson cleared her throat from the schoolhouse door. "Are you three planning on rejoining us?"

Bone carefully slid the brown paper into her pocket.

22

AFTER SCHOOL, BONE FOUND UNCLE ASH and Miss
Spencer rocking in the chairs on the porch of the Scott Brothers'
store, just like old times. Uncle Ash had his boots on the porch
railing. Miss Spencer sipped an RC Cola. Bone plopped down on
the milk crate between them. Uncle Ash handed her a grape Nehi.
The dogs stayed in the truck, and Bone couldn't blame them.

"We made some more calls," Uncle Ash said as he flipped
the cap off his Dr Pepper with his pocketknife. He checked to
see if anyone was in earshot. "Still didn't find any dog tags, but
India did figure out where *he* probably came from."

Bone turned to the professor.

"Near me!" she said, still amazed. "First your uncle called
someone he knew at Camp Pickett."

Uncle Ash leaned in. "The Brits asked the US to take thousands of Germans captured in North Africa. They started arriving a few months ago, going to camps all over the country. Including one in Mason's Cove in Catawba." He took a long drink of his pop.

"That's just a few miles from my college. Then I remembered a couple of weeks ago, the army was searching campus for someone. They wouldn't say who."

"An escaped prisoner?" Bone asked, though she knew the answer.

"He probably walked off a work detail," Uncle Ash explained. His friend at Camp Pickett said the prisoners were picking fruit in orchards and digging the new reservoir.

That made sense. Catawba wasn't that far away as the crow flies. Beck could've hitched a ride—or hopped a coal or freight train to get to Big Vein. Even if he walked the whole way, he could've been here in a few days.

Uncle Ash and Miss Spencer clinked their pop bottles together—and took long, congratulatory drinks.

"Well, I found his dog tag." Bone raised her grape Nehi.

Uncle Ash almost spit out his pop.

"But it's not like the one you have," she added. She was sure it belonged to the German.

Uncle Ash pulled out his tag and Beck's.

Bone didn't even have to look. "Nope, this one was bigger and with a line down the middle, like you could snap it in half."

Uncle Ash smacked his forehead. "Of course, he would have

gotten a new tag when he rejoined the army. Ours look different for this war, too."

"How do you know it was his?" Miss Spencer asked. "Did it have his name on it?"

"No." Bone hesitated and then pulled out the piece of brown paper she'd written the numbers and letters on. "It just had this on it."

Uncle Ash studied her pencil scratchings a bit. "This could be his service number, and this one his unit. The 'pz' probably stands for panzer. That's German for tank."

"How are you sure it's *his*?" Miss Spencer pressed.

Bone looked at Uncle Ash.

"Bone has a Gift—like mine, but not like mine," he said simply.

"Oh," Miss Spencer replied and didn't press it further.

Uncle Ash had told her about the Gifts! Bone couldn't tell if Miss Spencer believed him or not. Mamaw always said it was only knowledge for family and loved ones. *Oh.*

"Let's just say her method of knowing wouldn't be accepted in a court of law—but it's a powerful Gift." He clinked his bottle against Bone's. "Who had this tag?"

"Robbie Matthews."

Uncle Ash's boots slid clean off the railing.

She explained how she'd egged Robbie into bringing in some of his father's souvenirs.

"This changes things, don't it?" Uncle Ash pushed the brim of his hat back before polishing off his Dr Pepper.

Miss Spencer looked quizzically at them. "Who?"

"His father is the mine superintendent. And Robinson Matthews never did fight in the Great War at all." Uncle Ash explained how Mr. Matthews's father had gotten him a cushy posting as a supply clerk in Washington, DC, and he had a reputation for wheeling and dealing "souvenirs" with clerks on the front lines.

"Maybe he bought the tag from someone—or found it," Miss Spencer said.

"True. I never figured he had the sand to fight—let alone kill—someone." He whispered the last part, nodding at Mrs. Linkous as she walked into the store. "Did you get a chance to see anything . . . useful?" he asked Bone.

She knew what he meant. Did she see who killed Beck? She shook her head. "Robbie is bringing the tags to the dance. I wanted another chance to look at it."

"Oh, is he?" Uncle Ash ran his fingers through his hair. "I may have to make another call."

"But what about Uncle Junior?" Bone asked. Or Daddy? Or Will? Bone wanted to find out the man's story but not at the expense of their jobs. But then there was Tiny.

Uncle Ash thought on it as he lit, smoked, and fieldstripped a Lucky Strike. "We've got to do this for Tiny, but I'll warn Junior first."

That was fair.

23

THE CONVERSATION WITH UNCLE JUNIOR evidently wasn't going well. The brothers shouted at each other in the parlor. Mrs. Price, Miss Spencer, and Miss Johnson tried to drown them out with running water and loud gossip over the dishes. And Bone shivered out on the back porch as she filled in Will—and the boys—quietly on what she'd discovered.

She pinky swore Jake and Clay into silence. She didn't tell them how she knew certain things—and they didn't ask.

"Beck probably got off the train and hid while the night shift was loading the coal," she concluded.

"Then he surprised whoever was stealing it," Clay added.

"And wham!" Jake mimicked swinging a shovel.

Bone shivered again. This time she punched Jake in the arm.

But that was what happened, near as she could figure. And then a mine truck full of coal raced away, with its lights off.

She could put most of the pieces together: how Beck got there and what happened when he did. But the whodunit part was still fuzzy. And something . . . actually two somethings were bothering her about the tipple and that truck.

"Wouldn't the night shift notice if a truck was loaded up after the train?" Bone asked. The tipple was noisy, deafening even if you were underneath it. Somebody would've heard it running if it wasn't supposed to be.

Will and the boys exchanged a look. Then Will nodded. "The outside man would."

The outside man on the night shift was Tiny Sherman. No, not Tiny. He couldn't have.

"Tiny wouldn't be part of something like this," Clay said, echoing Bone's thoughts.

"Wouldn't need to be," Will said. He'd been thinking about this, she could tell. He tapped his little notebook. "Paperwork."

"Of course!" Jake said, nodding. "Daddy would load anything as long as the paperwork was in order." He explained how he'd helped his father keep track of the orders. The papers said how many car or truckloads were going out and what size coal to put in them.

So Tiny could've loaded that truck just as part of his job, not knowing someone was stealing it, as long as he had the paperwork. Bone felt relieved about that. Something else was still niggling at her, though.

"When y'all load the trucks, is there usually a mess?" Bone asked. That was the other part that didn't make sense.

Jake and Clay both shook their heads. "Not when Daddy runs the tipple, leastwise," Jake added.

"Mr. Matthews blamed Tiny, didn't he?" Bone said. "Could he have hit the wrong switch and dumped too much coal in the truck?" Mr. Sherman was new at running the tipple.

"You could fill up the hopper for a train car—and dump it on a truck, but—" Clay started laughing.

"But you'd bury the truck," Jake finished for him.

"Train car holds about eighty tons. The dump truck," Will squinted as he figured, "maybe holds twenty, give or take."

"We didn't shovel no sixty tons of coal before school." Clay laughed again.

"Could the tipple miss the truck by just a tetch?" Bone held her thumb and forefinger an inch or so apart.

The boys considered it.

"Yeah, if the truck parked too far forward," Jake allowed. "But most of the regular drivers been doing this for years."

"And they'd get docked if'n their loads were light," Clay added. His older brothers had driven trucks before they'd gone into the navy.

"Unless it wasn't one of the regulars," Bone said. Somebody new—or maybe not even on the payroll of the Superior Anthracite company—had been driving that truck the night Beck died. But he must have had help. While that truck was racing away, somebody dragged the body down into the mine, somebody who didn't know lime from rock dust. And that somebody took one of the German's dog tags or it got yanked off in the struggle. And that dog tag ended up in Mr. Matthews's collection.

The boys seemed to follow her thoughts.

"Those numbers you wrote down," Clay whispered. "From the dog tag."

"Criminy," Jake said.

"I gave them to Uncle Ash. The army should be able to identify the man from that. But that's what my uncles are fighting about."

The front door jangled and slammed shut, and the house behind them grew quiet. The only sound was the distant chugging of a train coming toward Big Vein.

Bone and the boys watched two flashlight beams make their way up the mine road—toward the tipple. Will tapped his watch: 8:13 p.m.

Uncle Ash was taking Junior to see the ghost dog.

Bone told the boys her plan to get another look at the tag.

24

BONE DIDN'T HEAR EITHER JUNIOR OR ASH come in that night. In the morning, Uncle Junior was already at work, as usual, by the time Mrs. Price rapped on Bone's door.

Did they decide to call the army? Should she go ahead with her plan? Bone pulled on her britches and sweater. The sweater was no help. She needed to see the rest of Beck's story, to see who really killed him. For Uncle Ash. For Mr. Sherman. She couldn't let the story smother and die like the man had. Like Uncle Ash almost did.

As Bone came down the back stairs, she heard Aunt Mattie, of all people, in the kitchen.

"Mother is helping out that Sherman woman again today," she said, clearly peeved at the idea.

"Oh law, I hope she stays safe," Mrs. Price said, shaking her head. "I heard that *certain people* are planning a visit to Sherman's Forest before Christmas," she added in a hushed tone.

Bone peered into the kitchen, feeling sick to her stomach. The Klan was planning to burn a cross, or worse, in Aunt Queenie's community. What if her plan didn't work?

"Them getting a Richmond lawyer just riled up the wrong element," Aunt Mattie chided. She sat at the kitchen table, impatiently stirring her coffee.

"Good morning, sunshine," Mrs. Price called extra loud from the ironing board. Wiping her hands, she pulled a plate of scrambled eggs and toast out from the oven and placed it in front of Bone.

"Mother asked me to help you get ready for the dance tonight," Aunt Mattie said stiffly, looking Bone up and down, just like old times.

Mrs. Price snorted. Aunt Mattie ignored her.

"I don't need your help," Bone told Mattie. Thinking about dresses—with Aunt Mattie—was the last thing she needed today. Bone plopped down in front of her eggs.

Mrs. Price retrieved a white-and-yellow polka-dot dress from the ironing board. Holding it up, she told Bone, "I finished taking in this one of your mother's. It'll look lovely with your sweater." She held it up to the yellow.

It did look lovely. Mama had worn both to church in the spring.

166

"She cannot wear white after Labor Day, Lydia!" Aunt Mattie touched the hem of the white dress and almost smiled. "Willow wore this when she was courting Bayard." Mattie disappeared into the memory—and then shook herself. "She wore this in the *summer*. You can have one of Ruby's old dresses. Something more appropriate to catch a beau."

"No, thank you!" Aunt Mattie was always trying to fix her, and Bone was not having it anymore. "I'm not looking for a beau—or your help." She yanked the dress away from her aunt. Mattie rose up from the table as if she were going to launch into Bone with one of her tirades. Bone beat her to it. "I tried to make nice with you months ago, you know, after you tried to drown me in your bathtub and all." Her voice caught. "But you've done your level best to either take potshots at me or ignore me since then. Uncle Ash asked me to declare a truce with you for Christmas—even though you treat him awful. Then when you thought he was dead, you couldn't wait to bury him! You didn't even want to sit with us at the funeral or let his friends from Sherman's Forest into the church. Then you had the gall to get mad at Uncle Ash when it turned out Mamaw and me were right. That it wasn't him after all!" She handed the dress back to Mrs. Price and pulled her sweater tight around her. She saw Mama putting the butter-yellow sweater over her ailing sister. "I wanted to tell you the story of this sweater." Bone's voice caught again. She took a deep breath and looked Aunt Mattie in the eye. "You still blame Uncle Ash for Mama. Truth is Mama loved you enough to die for you. But I've had enough.

"Thank you," she told Mrs. Price. Bone sat back down to eat her eggs, determined not to look at her aunt.

Aunt Mattie stood motionless, almost hanging in the air for a long moment. Then she disappeared out the back door without a word.

～～

The dance wasn't as fancy as past ones. Of course, with the war on and Uncle Henry gone, it wasn't a surprise. Only a few streamers hung from the rafters of the church hall. But it smelled like Christmas. Real holly branches and pine cones decorated the tables spread around the edge of the dance floor. The long folding tables near the front were laden with Christmas cookies and cakes. Everyone had saved up their sugar rations for tonight. Christmas music poured out of the big speakers on the floor. And there was actually a Christmas tree in the corner this year after all.

Bone adjusted her white-and-yellow polka-dot dress, her legs feeling positively naked, and straightened her butter-yellow sweater. Will had on his brown Sunday suit and a red tie. He tugged at the too-short sleeves.

"You clean up real nice." Jake elbowed her. Clad in his Sunday best, too, Jake was escorting his little sister, Joan.

"You look like a scarecrow," Clay said to Will—who promptly socked him in the arm.

Joan ran off to join her friends by the Christmas tree. Santa (aka Mr. Scott) usually left some candy or small presents for the little ones under the tree every year.

"Keep an eye peeled for Robbie," Bone told the boys.

"Don't worry. We know what to do," Clay reassured Bone.

"Look, cake!" Jake exclaimed. He and Clay made a beeline toward the dessert table. Ruby sliced them each a big hunk of stack cake.

Will mimed drinking and nodded toward the punch. And he was off, too.

A Glenn Miller tune played over the speakers. It was one of Daddy's favorites. Bone circled the hall watching. Aunt Mattie glumly doled out cups of punch. Bone refused to look at her. The Linkous twins twirled the Slusser sisters around on the floor. The boys ate cake and talked football. Miss Johnson and Miss Spencer sipped coffee at one of the tables. But there was no sign of Uncle Junior or Uncle Ash.

Robbie Mathews burst into the room—until a deep voice behind him told him to slow down. It was his father. Another first. Dadgummit. How was she going to do this? She eyed the side door. It led out to the little area between the church and the hall.

Robbie caught Bone's eye and patted his pocket, throwing a quick glance toward his daddy. Robbie had a corsage tucked in his other pocket, and he about stuck Ruby trying to get the corsage on. With a little help from Mamaw, he succeeded in pinning it to Ruby's green-and-red dress. Mr. Matthews glanced at Bone and then smiled at Aunt Mattie as she approached him with a cup of punch.

"Observing the little stories as they play out?" Miss Spencer appeared at Bone's side with an extra cup of punch. "You know that's what writers do."

So do detectives. She took the fruit punch and sipped it as she scanned the room.

"Your uncle and I have been talking about you. You could be a writer or maybe even a historian."

Miss Spencer and Uncle Ash had been doing a lot of talking.

"Where is Uncle Ash?" Bone asked.

"He'll be here soon. He said he had to see a man about a dog first."

Of course, someone's dog was probably ailing or hurt. He couldn't turn down a sick animal. But Bone sure wished she knew what he and Junior decided.

"You've got a gift for stories, he says. And doing the right thing. Like your uncle."

Was Miss Spencer trying to tell her something? Or was Uncle Ash?

"Um, Bone." Miss Spencer pointed. "Someone is trying to get your attention."

"Bone!" Jake not so subtly called her. The boys were gathered around Robbie at a table near the side exit, their backs to Robbie's dad. Clay socked Jake in the arm. "Ow!"

Even Aunt Mattie noticed. She glared at Bone as she made

her way to the table. Bone glared right back. Mattie kept watching as Mr. Matthews, who hadn't missed a beat, droned on at Mattie about something or other.

Bone pushed in between Will and Clay. Robbie had laid out a glittering array of medals and dog tags. He deployed several comic books to cover the booty when anyone walked by and peered too closely.

"What's that one?" Clay asked, pointing to a medal with a cross dangling from it.

"Daddy won it for bravery!" Robbie really believed it. He wanted his daddy so desperately to like him that he would believe anything that man said—and wanted everyone else to believe it, too.

"You don't say!" Jake elbowed Bone. "What did he do?"

Robbie launched into a long story about his daddy's company fighting a battle with the Germans. Bone scanned the table as Robbie told them how his daddy snuck around their lines and picked them off from the back one by one. Just like wild turkeys. The tale sounded suspiciously like that Gary Cooper movie, *Sergeant York*. This time Will elbowed her—then slipped a napkin-wrapped something into her hand. The dog tag. Even through the paper, she could feel it was Beck's. The woman. The children. The dogs. They were all older but still the same. Bone backed slowly away from the table toward the side exit. As she did, she tipped the punch onto her dress. "Sorry Mama," Bone whispered.

"Dang it!" Bone dabbed the punch with the napkin. "I'll be right back."

Robbie kept on talking. Aunt Mattie called out something about getting the club soda.

Bone slipped out the side door into the cool breeze. She could breathe again. She sat on the little steps outside. This is where the men came to smoke after church, out of sight. She unwrapped the tag amidst the stench of old cigar butts and held it up to the dim porch light. Music seeped through the door. And train brakes ground against the rail down below as the 8:15 inched through the tipple.

How did you get here? Bone saw him picking apples in an orchard. Behind him loomed the mountains with the unmistakable blue haze of home, *her* home, along its ridges. He ducked out through the woods, running until he reached train tracks. Following them, he stole clothes from a clothesline and buried his uniform by a creek. He walked along the tracks but hid as coal cars rumbled by, jumping onto an empty freight car. She felt his exhilaration as the Blue Ridge flew past him, smell of pines, road cuts streaked with coal and narrow bridges over flowing waters. The gentle rocking of the train lulled him to sleep. He awoke when the train's brakes screeched, slowing it onto a spur. Peering out into the night, Beck saw the brakeman's lantern illuminate the tiny sign by the switch: Big Vein. *His stop. Ash's home.* Beck buttoned up his coat and waited for the right moment to jump off. In the dark, the train rolled under the tipple, the machinery whirring to life. The wood and metal shaking and tumbling the coal down into the chutes, releasing a thunderous black rain. The train inched forward, brakes squealing, coal dropping. Again and again. Beck leapt to the hard ground and hid in the shadows of the tipple. After the train pulled away, he stepped out into the dim moonlight. A truck rolled up, and something hard swung down on Beck.

Who killed you?

"*Why did you do that?*" a strange voice asked.

"*He's just a bum, a hobo,*" a more familiar voice replied. Then Mr. Matthews peered down into Beck's face.

"*Nein, ich bin ein Soldat . . .*" Beck stammered.

The shovel hit him again and again. Blackness.

A hand gripped Bone's arm and yanked her to her feet.

"Where did you get this?" Mr. Matthews demanded.

It was only her and Mr. Matthews, and he peered down at her just as he had at Rainier Beck.

Her fist closed around the dog tag. She twisted her whole body, trying to break free of his grip.

"Answer me!"

"Robbie," Bone said, hoping he'd let her go. He didn't.

"Damn that worthless boy," Mr. Matthews said, his grip tightening on Bone's wrist. "I should've known he was pilfering my collection."

"You killed him!" Bone tried to stamp his foot—but she couldn't reach it.

"What?" His grip loosened a bit but not enough.

"*Nein, ich bin ein Soldat,*" she repeated.

Mr. Matthews dropped her arm, staggering back. He stared at her, his face blank. Then it darkened—and he lurched for her.

Bone dodged him. He was blocking the way back into the church hall.

Bone darted toward the road. Down below, the 8:15 was pulling away from the tipple.

She hadn't thought this part through.

What do I do?

The tag showed her. The black dog with saucer eyes.

She ran toward the tipple, Mr. Matthews panting behind her.

⟿

The ghost dog wasn't there.

She *really* hadn't thought this part through.

Still, she stood in the spot under the tipple where Rainer Beck had, his dog tag burning into her palm. It felt like a no-man's-land between the living and the dead, light and dark. Razor wire all around.

Mr. Matthews came to a wary stop a few yards before her, breathing hard, not daring to stand where she did. She saw flashes of the wife, the kids, the dogs, the towering glass buildings, all the things Beck loved. Tanks rolled through the desert, explosions falling everywhere. Surrendering. Escaping. He only had thoughts of fleeing into the hills to wait out the war—and maybe visiting an old friend along the way.

Tell the story, the object was telling her.

So Bone did. "This is where you killed Rainer Beck." She held up the tag. "A major in a panzer division."

"An escaped Nazi?" Mr. Matthews laughed. "No one will blame me for that! Give me the tag!"

He was right about that. The sheriff and army might not care about a POW who died while escaping. Beck had fought against Daddy in the desert. And the Nazis were doing awful, despicable things. Maybe she should let Mr. Matthews get away with it. Bone shook her head. He'd killed a man and framed someone else for it. Is that why he'd promoted Tiny in the first place? So he could blame Tiny if anyone found out what he was up to? Bone spat in the dirt in front of Mr. Matthews.

"You killed him because he saw you skimming coal—and you were happy to blame Uncle Ash and Tiny Sherman for it all." *The missing ball cap in his collection.* "You even planted that Memphis Red Sox cap in shaft twenty-seven!"

"Bone!" It was Aunt Mattie of all people, running toward them. She stopped by Mr. Matthews and turned on him. "Is that true?" she demanded.

He didn't answer her. "Just give me the damn dog tag, you runt!" He started toward Bone again.

Aunt Mattie threw herself in front of Bone. "Don't touch a hair on her head!" she snapped. "Answer my question!" She wagged a bony finger in his face.

Bone was impressed with Mattie's ferocity.

"Stay out of this, you old biddy!" He pushed Aunt Mattie to the ground and grabbed for Bone.

Aunt Mattie screeched—and so did the barn owl.

And then the ghost dog emerged from the shadows, its big saucer eyes fixed on the man.

Mr. Matthews went white and stumbled back.

The dog stood by Bone's side, baring its moon-white teeth.

Aunt Mattie gasped. "Move away, Bone, that dog looks rabid."

"It's okay, Aunt Mattie. She's here for him." Bone pointed toward Matthews. The dog inched forward. "Answer the question."

The spirit dog growled a low unearthly rumble. It was a river of coal tumbling to the ground. It was the roar of a tank thundering into battle. It was the rattle of an old pickup truck climbing a mountain. It was all of them rolled into one.

"Spirit dogs can be bringers of justice—or death," Bone whispered. "I think she's leaving the choice up to you."

Mr. Matthews tried to back away and run.

The dog advanced, its pointy ears flattened and its teeth bared.

"I wouldn't go anywheres just yet, Rob," Uncle Ash said, stepping into the light. His own dogs cowered behind him. "Bone, Mattie, y'all all right? India saw you heading this way."

"I'll be damned," a man in uniform beside him whispered.

He reached for a sidearm, but Uncle Ash put a hand on his arm.

"That won't do no good," Uncle Ash told him.

Mr. Matthews turned every which way, looking to run.

Uncle Junior, the sheriff, and the deputy blocked him one way, Will and the boys—including Robbie—another. Uncle Ash and the uniformed man—a third. And the women—Mamaw, Ruby, and Miss Spencer—filled in all the gaps, mortar in the wall between him and freedom.

Matthews kept one eye on the ghost dog as he faced Bone. "I didn't mean to do it. He surprised us."

"Us?" the sheriff asked.

"Me and Norton—my cousin from Greensboro. He drove the truck. We've been selling coal down in North Carolina and dealing with other goods on the black market. No telling when coal will be rationed, too."

The spirit dog snapped at Mr. Matthews and then turned tail toward the mine, vanishing.

Bone saw the flashes from the tag. "You dragged him down in the mine—and bashed him again and again till he was unrecognizable. That wasn't no accident."

Matthews nodded.

"Daddy?" Robbie gasped. "Why?"

Even then, his father wouldn't look at him. Did the money mean more to him than Robbie? Or was he ashamed? Hard to tell.

The sheriff signaled his deputy to cuff the mine superintendent and lead him away.

Bone felt sorry for Robbie as he watched his father get into the sheriff's car. He turned out his pockets and threw the souvenirs on the slag pile.

Bone handed Beck's dog tag to the army man. He had an armband that said MP. "How did y'all get the army here?" she asked her uncles.

"Yes, why is the *military* police here?" The sheriff crossed his arms, clearly annoyed.

"You know, Al, the coal in this mine is under contract to the army." Uncle Junior nodded toward the MP. "The men and I did a little digging. We found fake invoices for coal shipments that never quite made it to the army arsenal in Radford. Matthews was stealing from the war effort."

"I've let my superiors know about the theft." The MP took off his cap and wiped his brow. "But I might have to leave whatever I just saw out of the full report."

"That's probably wise." Uncle Ash chuckled as he hugged Bone. "Forever Girl, remind me to never tell another devil dog story again."

"I'll do no such thing," Bone whispered.

Those stories were part of his story, now and forever.

25

COME CHRISTMAS EVE, the faded yellow pickup climbed down the road from Reed Mountain, Uncle Ash at the wheel and Bone and Corolla in the passenger seat. Snow flecked the windshield as Bone warmed her hands on Corolla. She'd wisely stayed in the cab while Uncle Ash, Will, and Bone had chopped down the enormous Virginia pine that had been strapped to the truck. Its tip hovered above the Chevy's cab with its trunk secured to the bed of the pickup.

Uncle Ash slid open the little window behind them, letting in a blast of cold pine-scented air. "You hanging on back there?"

All Bone could see was a forest of green in the back. A gloved hand fought its way through the branches to give them a thumbs-up. Wrapped in a blanket—and no doubt warmed by the big dogs—Will was making sure the tree stayed strapped to the bed of the truck as they picked their way down the curvy mountain road. Uncle Ash slid the window shut.

"There's something for you in the glove box," Uncle Ash said as he handed her his work gloves. "And get us some peppermint sticks out, too."

Bone undid the flap and fished out the packet of peppermints and a small package done up in snow-white paper and tied in a red ribbon. Uncle Ash relieved her of the candy.

"I got that in Roanoke for you."

Bone undid the ribbon and ripped through the paper. Underneath was a leather-bound book with a tree tooled onto the front. She caught a flash of a young woman lovingly sewing the binding in a barn amid saddles and tack and hay bales.

"This lady at India's college makes them. She's the head groom, and I looked at one of the mares for her."

The book smelled of fresh leather and saddle soap, with just a hint of horse. Bone cracked open the cover and riffled through the pages—all blank.

"You can write down stories, you know, like Miss Spencer does, so they won't be lost . . ." Uncle Ash held a peppermint stick between his fingers like he was going to smoke it. "India is trying to get me to cut down on the Luckies." He took a pretend puff. "Not quite the same."

Bone inhaled the book's aroma again, this time catching a

hint of peppermint and tobacco, both of which Uncle Ash kept in the glove box. The paper smelled new. It was almost too fine to write on, but Bone had an overwhelming desire to set down story after story—though maybe not the kinds Miss Spencer was preserving.

"That's a laurel on the front, by the by."

It was her story book. For her Gift.

"Uncle Ash, I now know what my Gift is for. It tells me real stories that ought not be forgotten. Beck's. Will's daddy's. Mama's. And a thousand others." Bone was itching to start filling the creamy white pages. She was also scared that she couldn't do them justice, the pages or the stories.

Uncle Ash took a long drag on his peppermint stick. "You know, Forever Girl, you were mighty brave to tell Beck's story the way you did. It helped Tiny—and me." He pointed the stick at her. "Seems to me your Gift is more than just *preserving* those stories."

It's about making sure those voices get heard. That's what Uncle Ash was saying, and Bone knew he was right. Mamaw had shown her the family book where generations of Reeds recorded their Gifts. Very few had hers. Fewer still put her Gift to good use.

"Beck sent you this poetry book, you know." Bone pulled it out of her coat pocket and slid it back into the glove box.

"I know." Uncle Ash smiled. "Thank you, Forever Girl."

He turned up the radio as it started to play "White Christmas." He crooned awfully along with it, and they tried to out-croon

181

each other all the way to Big Vein. The tip of the tree bobbed in time with the music.

～∘～

They were still singing when they pulled to a stop in front of the boardinghouse.

"You are pert near a Popsicle," Bone exclaimed as Will and the dogs clambered out of the bed of the truck.

He stamped his feet on the ground to warm himself up.

Uncle Ash continued to sing as he cut the ties and handed the tree down to Bone and Will to drag up to the porch.

Will joined in with a surprisingly deep, off-key baritone that made Bone's eyes go wide—and Corolla and other dogs howl along with them.

"What in God's green earth is that racket?" Uncle Junior called to them as they dragged the tree toward the porch. He and Ivy's husband were stacking firewood out front for the bonfire. "You got a visitor." He pointed to the white '37 LaSalle coupe parked nearby.

A man in a dark gray overcoat climbed out of the driver's seat and strode toward them. "Mr. Reed? Ash Reed?" The man stretched out his hand. "Oliver Hill."

Uncle Ash promptly dropped the top end of the tree and shook the lawyer's hand. "Is Tiny out yet? I ran by the jail this morning. The sheriff said he was still waiting to hear from the judge."

"Mr. Sherman remains incarcerated." Mr. Hill sighed. "It seems Mr. Matthews recanted his confession, at least partially, claiming duress. And he further claims my client was responsible for any and all crimes committed."

"That's absolutely crazy." Uncle Ash patted his coat pocket for a smoke. He only found another peppermint stick.

"He's a liar," Bone said. She'd seen him do it—albeit in a way that wouldn't stand up in court. But the ghost dog made Mr. Matthews confess—in front of the sheriff and the MP and other witnesses. Plus Mr. Matthews had the dog tag—and the ball cap, she was sure—in his collection.

"That's as may be, young lady." Mr. Hill pushed the brim of his hat back. "But the judge decided the allegations warranted further investigation."

"So Tiny stays in jail over Christmas?" Uncle Ash asked.

Mr. Hill nodded. "He wanted me to let you know. My office and I are confident we can get all charges dismissed, but I'll need to talk to everyone involved after Christmas."

"Of course." Uncle Ash shook his hand again. "Would you like to join us?"

Mr. Hill pulled his overcoat tight around him. "Mrs. Sherman has invited me to the services and a potluck at her church." He started toward his car.

"Mr. Hill," Bone called after him. He turned, looking at her expectantly. The lawyer needed to know about the other ball caps. It might help Tiny. "Mr. Matthews has a collection of

Negro League hats in his study. One's missing."

He raised an eyebrow. "Very interesting." He nodded at her. Then the lawyer slid back into the LaSalle and headed down the road.

"Damn," Uncle Ash muttered as he picked up the top of the tree again, his brow creased with worry. "Robeson Matthews sure is a peculiar one."

"Why did he collect all that stuff? He didn't serve in the war or even like black folks."

"He didn't like Tiny, leastways. Him and me tussled with the Matthews boys all the time when we were kids."

Bone recalled the black eye and busted lip she'd seen.

"They—Robeson especially—didn't like Tiny on account of him being such a good ball player." Uncle Ash shifted the tree to his other hand. "In fact, I bet Robeson was one of the boys who stomped Tiny's pitching arm. Tiny wouldn't never say, though, seeing as Robeson's father was a judge at the time."

"That's not fair," Bone protested. "They shouldn't have gotten away with that back then! And they shouldn't keep Tiny locked up now for something Mr. Matthews did."

"Bone, I'm not going to lie. It ain't fair." Uncle Ash set down the tree again. He handed Bone another peppermint stick. "Sometimes we do everything we can do—and it still don't work out exactly like we hoped." He took a deep breath of the crisp air. Snowflakes started gently falling. "But I got a good feeling Mr. Hill will be able to get Tiny out. And the army does not take kindly to war profiteers. Mr. Matthews will get his come-uppance—thanks in no small part to you, Forever Girl."

Bone couldn't help noticing Uncle Ash still looked a bit worried.

"Amen!" Will called from the back of the tree, which he was still holding. "Now can we get this thing in the house?"

Uncle Ash laughed and picked up his end again.

⁓

They dragged the tree into the front hallway of the boarding-house. The corner, in the crook of the front stairs, was the perfect spot for the tree. Only when they stood it up, its top bent a good foot under the ceiling. Bone laughed, feeling the echo of Mama's joy from the butter-yellow sweater on a Christmas Eve many years ago. The joy was dampened by the idea of Mr. Sherman spending the holidays in jail—but still there.

"You always get this part wrong," Aunt Mattie told Uncle Ash. She was laughing, but not in a mean way. Her voice was warm and full of memories.

Uncle Ash gripped his peppermint stick in his teeth as he shimmied under the tree to tighten the stand.

Will headed up the stairs, saw in hand. Bone busied herself with the box of ornaments on the hall table. Finding the sparkly silver star, she bounded up the stairs after Will. He started sawing.

"Oh, I get a lot of things wrong, sis," Uncle Ash declared as he crawled to his feet.

"Shh. I can't hear what they're saying," Bone whispered, pointing toward Ash and Aunt Mattie. Will stopped to listen, too.

Uncle Ash brushed the pine needles off his pants. He reached into his coat pocket and produced the packet of peppermint sticks, offering one to Mattie. "That's quite a brave thing you did standing up to Matthews—and a ghost dog."

Aunt Mattie harrumphed, but she took a peppermint stick. "Not sure which was worse."

Brother and sister stood there for a moment, each savoring the candy. Bone and Will exchanged a glance. She shrugged, and he started sawing ever so slowly.

Mattie finally spoke. "I couldn't bear to lose someone else I love," she said.

Will stopped sawing. Bone gulped. *Mattie loved her.*

"It don't make up for what I did to her." Aunt Mattie's voice caught.

Uncle Ash put an arm around her shoulder. "No, it doesn't," he said. "But it's a start."

"I'm glad we didn't lose you neither," she added quietly.

"I do believe that's the nicest thing you've said to me in forty-seven years." Uncle Ash laughed.

"Don't get used to it!" Aunt Mattie squirmed out from under his arm. "Might take me forty-seven more years to think of another nice thing to say."

Will sawed through the last bit of the treetop. "Timber!" he warned as it slipped out of his hand and tumbled toward the foyer floor. Uncle Ash gently pushed Mattie aside, but the foot of pine still narrowly missed her.

Bone braced herself as Aunt Mattie looked up at them, a flash of fury in her eyes. It soon gave way, though, to a hearty laugh. "This will look nice on our kitchen table." She scooped up the miniature tree and headed into the parlor without a backward glance.

"Well, don't that beat all?" Uncle Ash mumbled, more to himself than anyone, before he stepped out onto the front porch.

"Maybe old dogs can learn new tricks," Bone wondered aloud.

Will snorted. "Best not let her hear you say that."

As he held her steady, Bone leaned over the railing to place the star on top of the Christmas tree. The choir began singing "O Holy Night" over at the church.

And thus began the Christmas truce of 1942.

~ ⁓ ↄ

For the rest of Christmas Eve, the boardinghouse bustled with people and dogs of the living variety. The smells of baking ash bread and simmering shuck beans with pork and the sounds of Bing Crosby on the radio filled the house. Ruby served the apple stack cake she'd whipped up. Mamaw hung stockings for all the grands with one orange in each. Bone regaled her audience with the ghost dog story by the bonfire. Uncle Ash told the one about the haunted mirror over in Radford. Mamaw told one about a shack haunted by a skeleton cat. Then they clanged pots and pans together at midnight to ward off the dead.

No animals talked. The dogs didn't kneel—except for Corolla, who Uncle Ash had taught to beg for Christmas cookies. But the elder bush did bloom by the front door.

And Uncle Ash got a letter from a dead man. The worn envelope bore the postmarks of its long journey from Catawba to New York and back to Big Vein. Uncle Ash explained that the army had to read and censor every POW's mail. Inside, the letter bore a censor stamp, but nothing was blacked out. It simply said, "You were right. I should've followed my own lights."

EPILOGUE

THE COLD, WINDY DAY was perfect for a cleansing, Mamaw said, as she handed Bone the box of white vinegar, rags, and newspapers. Bone knocked on the front door of the parsonage, box in hand. The sound echoed inside. Uncle Ash and Junior had loaded up the last of the furniture this morning and were moving it into Mattie's new place in Radford. Ruby was supervising.

"Come in, Mama," Aunt Mattie yelled from the back.

Bone pushed the door open and set the supplies on the kitchen counter. The place looked hollowed out. "It's me," she called.

Aunt Mattie emerged from the bedroom, broom in hand. Her hair was up in a kerchief and she was wearing an old shirt and rolled-up trousers. She looked down at herself and laughed.

"They were Henry's. I couldn't throw everything of his away. Is Mama coming?"

"Nope. I'm here to help you clean."

Aunt Mattie cracked a smile. "Okay, then." She handed Bone the broom. Mattie grabbed a bottle of vinegar and a stack of newspapers from the box. "I'll do the windows." She started toward the front room and paused. "I hear Tiny finally got out."

Bone nodded. "Yesterday." Mr. Hill, it turned out, was a very good lawyer. It still made Bone furious, though, that the sheriff and judge had to be convinced Tiny was innocent—even after Mr. Matthews confessed and the army charged him with profiteering.

"Good," Aunt Mattie said. "He's a good man."

Bone started at the back of the house. In Uncle Henry's study, with the dust and dirt, she swept out the memories of him reading his dime-store novels instead of writing his sermon. Of her lying awake on the cot, telling Ruby about Ashpet while Mattie and Henry fought over him going off to war.

In the hallway, she scrubbed away the memory of finding Mama's sweater hidden in the shed. Of standing up to Mattie, and her ripping the sweater off and dragging her down the hall to the bathroom. In there, Bone studied the clean tub, still able to taste the iron-cold bathwater as Mattie held her head under. Bone swept every speck of dust from the black-and-white tiles.

In the big bedroom, Bone could still see Mattie asleep in the bed, the butter-yellow sweater draped over her, and Mama slumped in the chair. Dead. Uncle Ash crying at her feet.

Bone swept with a fury, fighting back the tears. She swept out the hurtful memories. The unkind remarks. The loss.

Aunt Mattie crept into the room, newspapers and vinegar in hand. Bone whipped the pine boards with the broom. Mattie scrubbed the big window until it squeaked and the smell of vinegar filled the air. Then she flung the window open. Bone wiped her eyes on the sleeve of Mama's sweater. She'd come to this house back in September, ready to tell Aunt Mattie the sweater's story, really the story of Mama and the sister she saved. Aunt Mattie wasn't ready to hear it then. Bone watched her aunt's shoulders tremble as she stood in the fresh air.

"I'm ready to hear that story now," Aunt Mattie whispered.

It came bursting out of Bone like a gale-force wind.

As it poured out, Aunt Mattie threw open the rest of the windows in the room. Cold gusts carried off the lingering ghosts, leaving the parsonage and more New Year's fresh and clean.

Aunt Mattie wiped her eyes on her shirtsleeve and held her arms out to Bone.

Maybe this truce would last. Maybe it would become a peace, at least until the next war started.

Author's Note:

Just like the other stories in the Ghosts of Ordinary Objects series, *The Truce* relies on a mixture of history and folklore and/or ghost stories. Though I'm not a historian, I do try my best to get the history (and folklore!) right. Here's a little backstory on some of the history and stories used in this book.

LOCAL POW CAMPS

Just as Ash explained to Bone, the US agreed to house POWs in America starting in 1942. The first POWs came from Rommel's Afrika Korps, elite German tank battalions fighting in North Africa. POW camps were quietly spread across our country, and the prisoners helped make up for a shortage of labor on the home front. They picked fruit, built buildings, farmed, and so forth. Approximately 425,000 German prisoners lived in 700 camps spread throughout the United States during the war.

One of those camps was located in Mason's Cove near what's now called Hollins University in Roanoke, Virginia; today, the camp is called Ward Haven Camp and Retreat. In the 1930s, the camp was originally built for the Civilian Conservation Corps. In 1941, the army used it as a mechanical training school where soldiers learned to work on trucks and other vehicles. In 1942, it welcomed its first German POWs. The camp housed around 150 prisoners until 1945.

I always seem to find out the really interesting stuff *after* I write the first draft. Evidently, my uncle's cousin actually encountered a runaway German POW from the Mason's Cove camp. Having walked off a work detail, the POW knocked on this cousin's door, looking for food. The cousin, naturally, called the police, and the POW was returned to the camp. No German POWs, to my knowledge, made it as far as McCoy (the real Big Vein). But they could've since the whole area is connected by coal and freight train tracks.

In fact, not many German POWs tried to escape, and those that did, didn't get far. Per the Geneva Convention, prisoners were given similar quarters to our military and paid for their labor. By many reports, the average German soldier had it better in an American POW camp than they did at home or in their own army. Many of the POW camps out west even offered college degrees. Some more militant Nazis did try to make trouble for their fellow prisoners whom they saw as collaborating with the enemy. These prisoners were sent to more secure facilities.

WYTHEVILLE LYNCHING

The lynching case Mamaw refers to really did happen. In 1926, Raymond Byrd was lynched in Wytheville, Virginia, which is approximately fifty miles from where this book is set. Mr. Byrd was accused of rape, though the alleged victim denied it, and was arrested. A mob of white men shot Raymond Byrd in his jail cell and then dragged him through town and out to the farm of the woman he supposedly raped. There, he was hanged from a tree.

The last "documented" lynching in Virginia, Raymond Byrd's case spurred the state's 1928 anti-lynching law—as well as the flight north for many black people in Wythe County.

OLIVER HILL

Oliver Hill was a noted African American civil rights attorney from Richmond, Virginia. He began practicing law in Roanoke during the Great Depression. By the early 1940s, he'd established his own law firm with two other prominent African American lawyers in Richmond. Hill did work with the NAACP during this time period, but, to my knowledge, he didn't take criminal cases. His legal career focused on ending "separate but equal." Hill worked for equal pay, voting rights, access to education and transportation, among other things. One of his cases—*Davis v. County School Board of Prince Edward County*—became one of the five cases decided by the US Supreme Court under *Brown v. Board of Education*. This landmark ruling established that racial segregation in schools was unconstitutional. Mr. Hill continued to practice law and work for civil rights for many decades after that. He won numerous awards, including the Presidential Medal of Freedom. He died in 2007. Several courthouses, buildings, and streets are named after him.

GHOST DOG STORIES

All of the ghost stories used in this book—except for the Greenbrier ghost—came from sources such as *Virginia Folk*

Legends, the book of stories compiled by Works Progress Administration workers in Virginia. However, many more ghost dog tales are told throughout the Appalachian South. An excellent source is *Ghost Dogs of the South* by husband and wife folklorists Randy Russell and Janet Barnett.

GREENBRIER GHOST

The Greenbrier ghost story is a famous (and true) case that has been the subject of many books. Her story is even on a state highway marker. On January 23, 1897, Elva Zona Heaster Shue was found dead by a neighbor boy at the bottom of the stairs in her home in Lewisburg, West Virginia. Her death was thought to have been from natural causes—until Zona's ghost appeared to her mother. The ghost described how she'd been killed by her husband. The mother got her daughter's body exhumed and the autopsy corroborated Zona's story. It's still the only case in our judicial system where a ghost helped solve her own murder. Her husband was convicted and sent to prison, where he died.